A Pocketful of EYES

D1634447

700040015967

A Pocketful of EYES

Lili WILKINSON

ALLEN&UNWIN

First published in 2011

Copyright © Lili Wilkinson 2011

All rights reserved. No part of this book may be reproduced or transmitted in any form or by any means, electronic or mechanical, including photocopying, recording or by any information storage and retrieval system, without prior permission in writing from the publisher. The *Australian Copyright Act 1968* (the Act) allows a maximum of one chapter or ten per cent of this book, whichever is the greater, to be photocopied by any educational institution for its educational purposes provided that the educational institution (or body that administers it) has given a remuneration notice to Copyright Agency Limited (CAL) under the Act.

Allen & Unwin
83 Alexander Street
Crows Nest NSW 2065
Australia
Phone: (61 2) 8425 0100
Fax: (61 2) 9906 2218
Email: info@allenandunwin.com
Web: www.allenandunwin.com

A Cataloguing-in-Publication entry is available from
the National Library of Australia

www.trove.nla.gov.au

ISBN 978 1 74237 619 6

Cover photos by Britt Erlanson/Getty Images; Larry Lilac/Alamy; iStockphoto
Cover and text design by Lisa White
Set in 12/18 pt Adobe Garamond Pro by Bookhouse, Sydney
Printed and bound in Australia by the SOS Print + Media Group.

10 9 8 7 6 5 4 3

MIX
Paper from
responsible sources
FSC® C011217

The paper in this book is FSC certified.
FSC promotes environmentally responsible,
socially beneficial and economically viable
management of the world's forests.

For Michael,
who helped solve this mystery and many others

On entering the taxidermy laboratory in the Melbourne Natural History Museum's Department of Preparation on the morning of Thursday 13 January, at 9:25, Beatrice May Ross noticed six unusual things, all of which turned out to be of the utmost significance. The things (in no particular order) were:

1. The clock on the wall was three minutes slow, putting the time at 9:22.
2. On the third shelf from the right and four shelves down, a jar marked Eyes, Reptile, S–M was missing a lid.
3. Gus, the Head Taxidermist, was eating a wholemeal sandwich containing roast chicken, mayonnaise, alfalfa sprouts, plastic cheese, tomato and beetroot.

1

4. The beetroot was about to make a desperate bid for freedom and head for the neutral territory on the front of Gus's bottle-green Natural History Museum hoodie.
5. Gus didn't seem to be particularly concerned that Bee was running twenty-five minutes late (or twenty-two if you believed the clock on the wall).
6. There was a stranger in the laboratory.

The stranger was a young man, probably a couple of years older than Bee, and he was sitting at the spare desk next to Gus's. He had artfully messy dark-brown hair, black-framed glasses and a cheeky glint in his eye that made Bee feel immediately hostile.

Gus made no attempt to introduce Bee to the stranger, or acknowledge her presence in any way, so she went to her desk and sat down. The possum lay sprawled in exactly the same position as it had been when she left the building last night.

Why was there a *boy* in her laboratory? The spare desk had previously been piled high with seagull wings and ice-cream containers marked CLAWS and plastics catalogues. Now it was cleared, and the boy was sitting there. He wasn't... *working*, was he? Why did Gus want someone else? Did he think she wasn't doing a good enough job? Bee prodded the possum. Its fur was thick and stiff at the back, but it had a lovely soft fuzzy belly. Its blood, organs and bones had all been removed, leaving just skin and fur and claws and whiskers.

Bee glanced at the young man, who winked at her and grinned. Bee scowled and looked away. She and Gus had a *routine*. This new boy would ruin everything. She measured and snipped a piece of galvanised wire twice the length of the possum's torso, and bent it into a possumish shape, referring to the page of *Anatomy of Australian Mammals* open beside the possum. She tugged a handful of cottonwool from a large bag under her desk, then wrapped it tightly around the wire frame, making it thicker in the middle and tapering it off at either end. She held it up next to the possum and squinted, checking the book again, and marked the position of the shoulders, hips and tail with a black texta.

Gus was making notes in the exhibition plan folder on his desk. The new boy was bent over the emu that Gus had been working on, carefully threading wire into its neck and packing it tightly with cottonwool. He looked up, as if he could feel Bee's eyes on him. She quickly turned back to her possum. How come he got to work on the emu, instead of a boring old possum?

Bee had first visited the Museum of Natural History in Year Eight, on a science excursion. She'd loved its order and precision, and in Year Ten she'd returned to do her work-experience placement. Last year her science teacher had recommended her for an assistant job in the taxidermy department, and she'd started working with Gus after school and on weekends. She'd been there full time since school had finished in early December (with a week off for Christmas), and would stay until she started Year Twelve in February.

Bee loved working at the museum, so much that she didn't mind the long hours and rather token salary. Initially she had just fetched and carried for Gus and watched him work. He'd barely spoken to her for the first few weeks, except to grumble about the 'newfound nonsense' practices of covering polyurethane moulds with animal skins – he insisted on nineteenth-century techniques involving cottonwool and wire.

But they had an *understanding*, a shared appreciation of order and methodical attention to detail. Every morning they would work in companionable silence until eleven, when Bee would go upstairs and order two triple espressos from the museum café. Sometimes she bought a lamington or a vanilla slice for herself, but Gus only ever had coffee.

After Bee had gained Gus's trust (and, she hoped, a little of his grudging respect), he let her do bits and pieces of real work: finishing off a foot or a wing, or inserting a glass eye. The possum was her first solo project, and she thought it was turning out rather well.

The Department of Preparation was located underground, in the vaults of the Natural History Museum. These rooms were known as 'the Catacombs', and as well as the partially renovated taxidermy lab and the other preparatory studios, they comprised a rabbit warren of storerooms containing old display cases, disused stuffed animals, and lumps of rock that scientists of the early twentieth century had thought were meteorites, but had turned out to just be plain old rocks. The lab was always cool and quiet: a haven from the heat and bustle of summer, and the hot breath and sticky hands of the children who swarmed through the museum every day of the school holidays like grizzly, hyperactive locusts.

Best of all, Bee liked the laboratory because it was ordered. Neat and scientific. Each process straightforward and methodical. She was unperturbed by the animal carcasses – and their inevitable cycle of breakdown and decay. Death, after all, was a natural process. It was predictable, normal, everyday. Dead animals were far less mysterious than the messy unpredictability of living people. In the taxidermy lab, every mystery had an answer.

Mysteries had always been a big part of Bee's life. When she was little, she had wanted as much mystery as the day could contain. She was forever tapping on the walls of her brick-veneer suburban home, hoping for a panel to swing out and reveal a secret passage. She kept a meticulous diary full of observations of everything around her – in code, of course – down to the postman's arrival time, and the number of thick fantasy novels on her mother's bedside table. She observed and analysed. One just never knew what would later reveal itself as a clue. Bee had insisted that her mother call her Trixie – after wholesome girl-sleuth Trixie Belden – and she had carried a detective kit everywhere she went, containing a magnifying glass, a pair of rubber gloves, a notebook, a sharpened pencil, a battered Miss Marple novel and a lipstick, because, as Nancy Drew had taught her, lipstick wasn't just for glamour – it was also useful for writing SOS messages on windows and mirrors if one happened to find oneself locked in a room by a malicious and vengeful gardener, uncle or heir to a fortune.

But everyone had to grow up sooner or later, and by the time Bee was eleven, reality had sunk in. Real life bore no resemblance to Nancy Drew or Trixie Belden novels.

It was more like Ian Rankin or Raymond Chandler. Bee may have had a short-fuse quick temper like Trixie Belden, but the resemblance ended there. She didn't live in a sleepy town surrounded by beautiful autumnal woods and hidden caches full of jewels the way Trixie Belden did. And as for Nancy Drew, nobody could ever be as perfect as Nancy. She could paint, sew, cook and play bridge. She was fluent in French, and was a skilled dancer, musician and physician. And she could drive a motorboat or a car like a pro at the age of sixteen, not to mention fly a plane in heels, without messing up her hair. And all under the tender gazes of her rich, doting father and adoring boyfriend.

Bee frowned. What was Nancy's boyfriend's name? She could picture him in her head. He was tall and broad-shouldered and square-jawed and white-toothed. But what was his *name*?

'Toby,' said a voice in Bee's ear. She turned to see the new boy bent over her desk, examining her work.

'No,' she said, shaking her head. 'It wasn't Toby. It was...Todd or Brad or Ken or something.'

'What?' He squinted at her through his glasses.

Bee assessed him with a practised detective's eye. He was wearing an almost threadbare navy penguin polo shirt that looked to be from the eighties. Bee wondered

7

if it was expensive-trendy-vintage-shop second-hand, or the more noble op-shop second-hand. Either way, it was an excellent fit, and showed off well-shaped arms and a chest that was solid without being ripped. The boy clearly exercised, but wasn't a fitness junkie. Dumbbells at home, Bee guessed, and the occasional run. He almost certainly owned a bicycle.

The faint outline of stubble indicated that he shaved, and a red nick on the left side of his jaw suggested that he hadn't been doing it for long. His skin was generally clear, his eyelashes were thick and his brows were well-shaped. He smelled clean, like soap and boy-deodorant. She couldn't detect a tobacco odour on him, and although his cuticles and nails were disgracefully chewed, there was no evidence of nicotine staining.

He raised his eyebrows at her and Bee felt her face redden. He probably thought she was looking at him in an...appraising kind of way because she liked him. Not because she was a totally objective observer of human behaviours and characteristics.

'Nothing,' she said. 'Are you here to work on the exhibition too?'

He nodded. 'I'm a second-year med student,' he said. 'This is extra credit. You?'

Bee shrugged. 'Just a summer job. I'm starting Year Twelve in a couple of weeks.'

He grinned in that patronising *good luck* way that uni students had. Bee observed that he had excellent teeth, and surmised that he'd probably had some serious orthodontic intervention.

Behind them, Gus cleared his throat. It was a husky, rattling sound, as if he were clearing cobwebs that had been there since his birth, which Bee assumed was a very long time ago, as Gus was at least seventy. 'Those critters aren't going to stuff themselves,' he said, in his growly voice with the hint of an English accent.

The boy – Toby – rolled his eyes at Bee, and she smiled back, then immediately felt annoyed at herself. Gus's slice of beetroot finally escaped the confines of his sandwich, and planted itself firmly on the front of his hoodie. He swore, then gingerly picked the beetroot up between thumb and forefinger and ate it.

At 10:53 AM (or 10:50 by the lab's clock), Bee climbed the stairs leading from the Catacombs and stood outside in the sun for five minutes, clearing her head of preservation chemicals and irritating thoughts about Toby. The shock of being in the beating heat of summer was pleasant for about three of those five minutes, until Bee's jeans started to stick to her thighs. She pushed her sunglasses up her nose.

'Hot,' observed Toby, appearing beside her with a can of lemonade.

Bee had a personal policy of not replying to redundant statements, so she ignored him. She wondered absently what made him chew his cuticles so viciously. Anxiety? What did he have to be anxious about?

'You haven't told me your name,' he said.

Bee told him, abruptly, and wondered if today would be a vanilla slice day or a lamington day.

'That Gus is a bit of a character, hey?'

Bee sighed. Small talk was so mundane. She retreated into the blissful cool of the museum, and purchased two triple espressos from the café. She wasn't going to let Toby ruin her routine.

She walked back the long way through the exhibitions hall, instead of along the concrete staff-access corridors. The older sections of the museum – the Mollusc Room, the Hall of Native Flora, the Geology Exhibit – were not as popular with the children, so it was a reasonably peaceful walk. Bee liked looking at all the creatures, frozen in time and space with the help of wire, cottonwool and lots of chemicals.

In the Weights and Measurements display, a ruby-throated hummingbird perched on one side of a tiny set of scales, balanced on the other by two paperclips. It was overshadowed by the hulking grey mass of an African elephant, balanced on a much larger set of scales opposite a pinkish-grey replica of a blue whale's tongue.

As she passed the Red Rotunda, a small yet grand octagonal room painted in a rich vermilion, Bee heard voices and paused by the entrance. One of the tour guides was talking to an old man sitting in a straight-backed leather chair in the centre of the room.

'I'm so sorry to interrupt you, sir,' the tour guide said, sounding rather breathless. 'But I heard you introduce yourself at the front desk and I just wanted to tell you that I am a huge fan. Your research is so inspiring; you're a total hero in this place.'

Bee peered at the old man. He didn't look like a hero. Deep wrinkles carved lines and fissures into his face. His chin bristled with stubble, and thick white hair curled around his ears. His eyes were the palest blue, like the colour of a cloudless sky nearest the horizon at dawn. They were also watery and red-rimmed, as if he'd been crying, although Bee supposed that it was just the effects of age. And yet he looked sad, sadder than Bee had ever seen anyone. Maybe he had been crying after all.

'Dr Cranston?' the tour guide said. 'Are you okay?'

The man looked up, startled. It was as though he hadn't noticed the tour guide until then. Bee guessed he was around seventy years old.

'Fine, fine,' he said, standing up. 'I'm fine.'

'I'm sorry,' said the tour guide. 'I didn't mean to disturb you.'

'It's fine. I was just leaving.'

The old man pushed past the tour guide through the high wooden doorway of the Red Rotunda and marched past Bee. Bee watched him and decided that maybe he was a little younger. He didn't move like an old man.

The tour guide trailed slowly after him, adoration in his eyes.

As Bee made her way towards the stairs that led to the preparatory studios, she noticed a plaque on the wall outside the Red Rotunda.

THE CRANSTON COLLECTION WAS DONATED BY
DR WILLIAM CRANSTON, AO
SCIENTIST, ANATOMIST AND GENEROUS BENEFACTOR
OF THIS MUSEUM

'Huh,' said Bee, and returned to the taxidermy lab.

12

Gus was in a strange mood. In the four and a half months that Bee had been working at the museum, his conversation had been limited to how to fix and preserve an animal skin, how to measure and record its details, and how to mount and pose the finished specimen. Most of the time he was bent over his work, delicate tools in hand, a magnifying glass fixed to the desk on a posable metal arm.

Yet now he was laughing with Toby and eating a jam doughnut with chocolate icing and sprinkles.

'Did you know,' Toby was saying, 'that necrophilia wasn't a crime in the US until 1965?'

Gus assured Toby with a grin that in fact he had not known that.

'And even today it's only a crime in sixteen states. A woman in California stole a hearse, fled the state and was found in the back getting cosy with the corpse. And the only thing she was charged with was auto theft.'

'Extraordinary,' said Gus, shaking his head. Toby saw Bee and winked at her.

Gus looked up. 'My coffee!' he said. 'Marvellous. Have a doughnut? I bought a dozen.'

Bee handed over the coffee. Something very strange was going on.

'You can learn all sorts of things from a corpse,' Gus said, turning back to Toby. 'Its age, its lifestyle. Every detail about how it lived and died.'

Toby nodded. Bee went back to her desk, feeling as if her entire world had been turned upside down. Why was Gus eating a doughnut? He *never* had morning tea. Bee couldn't remember ever seeing him eat before today. And he'd already had a sandwich!

'Like Frankenstein's treasure map,' said Toby.

'*Well*,' said Gus. 'If you like Frankenstein, let me tell you about Charles Guthrie.'

'Who?'

'In 1908, in Missouri, Charles Guthrie became the first person to master anastomosis.'

'Ana-what?' said Bee, curious despite herself.

'Anastomosis,' Toby told her. 'The art of stitching one vessel to another without leaks.'

Gus nodded. 'Guthrie grafted a dog's head onto another dog.'

'No *way*!' said Toby.

Gus took another bite of doughnut. 'Chin to chin,' he said, through a mouthful of crumbs.

Bee felt a little sick. There was nothing orderly or methodical about two-headed dogs.

'The upside-down dog started to cry in pain after about five hours, and Charlie put them both down after seven.'

'Dude.'

'That's awful,' said Bee.

'That was only the beginning,' said Gus. 'In the Soviet Union in the fifties, scientists did more puppy-head transplants. Some of the puppies lived as long as twenty-nine days, and would eat and bark and try to bite their host dog.'

Bee shuddered, and was suddenly grateful that Gus hadn't spoken much before.

Gus continued to chuckle and tell off-colour stories all day. And eat. Bee had never seen anyone eat so much. He had two hamburgers with chips for lunch, along with a strawberry milkshake, then inhaled a Crunchie, two lamingtons and a slice of banana bread for afternoon tea, washing it down with a large hazelnut cappuccino with extra froth and chocolate sprinkles. Bee was aghast.

Even as Toby was chatting and joking with Gus, Bee could feel him watching her, as if he were attempting to get a reaction. He kept trying to catch her eye – and succeeding far too often. What did he *want*? Was he just being annoying? Or did he like her? Bee wasn't sure which option was worse. She just kept her head down and worked on her possum, clenching her jaw every time Gus laughed at something Toby said. Gus had never laughed with *her*. She and Gus didn't have a laughing relationship. They had a relationship based on respect and professionalism.

The main body of the possum was now shaped, and Bee was working on its front left leg. She poked a sharpened piece of wire through the pad of the animal's paw, and fed it through the limb to attach the body. She then turned the skin inside-out so she could wrap more cottonwool around the wire, as well as some thicker flax-string to stand in for the possum's muscles.

'So how long have you been working on this little fellow?' Toby asked, leaning over her.

'Not long,' she said, although in truth the possum had been hard going and it had taken her all week to get this far. 'I'll finish it by the end of the day,' she said.

Toby looked at the still rather limp furry body. 'No, you won't,' he said, matter-of-factly.

'I *will*!' said Bee. But there was still a lot of work to do. She imagined the smarmy look on Toby's face the next morning when he came into the lab. She was determined to prove him wrong.

Bee pulled out her phone and sent her mother a text message to say she'd be home late. She'd finish her possum. Even if she had to stay up all night.

16

2

GUS LEFT AT 8:37 PM, opening a packet of salt and vinegar chips on his way out. Bee fully expected Toby to bolt out the door as soon as Gus had gone, but to her surprise he stayed.

They didn't speak, just worked silently. The only sound was the *snip* of scissors and the faint squeaking of cottonwool.

At 9:09 PM, Bee's phone rang, making her jump. Her watch caught on a raw edge of possum fur and pulled one of her stitches free. She answered the phone, sliding her watch off and placing it on her desk.

'Are you on your way home?' her mother asked. 'Can you pick up a pizza?' Bee could hear familiar electronic beeps and whistles and metallic clanks in the background.

'Sorry,' she said. 'I'm still here.'

Toby looked over at her and grinned like an idiot. She turned her back on him.

'Never mind,' said Angela. 'I'll order in. Don't work too hard!'

'Was that your boyfriend?' asked Toby, as Bee slipped her mobile into her bag and turned her attention to the broken stitch.

Surely if she ignored Toby he'd leave soon.

He didn't.

ⓘ ⓘ ⓘ

Bee rubbed her eyes and glanced at the clock. It said 11:35 but it was still three minutes slow, so in fact it was 11:38. She glanced at Toby, who was bent over the head of the emu, carefully smoothing the stuffing around its neck. He must have felt her looking, because he spoke for the first time in two hours.

'An emu's hips are anatomically the closest thing in the animal kingdom to a human's.'

Bee blinked, not sure what to do with that piece of information. 'Do elderly emus have to get hip replacements?' she said at last.

Toby leaned back in his chair and smiled. 'Our heart is closest to that of a pig,' he went on. 'We have lungs like a goat, knees like a brown bear, and a brain similar to that of a six-month-old Jersey cow.'

'Really?' said Bee. 'How come I've never seen a Jersey cow win *Who Wants to Be a Millionaire?*'

Toby shrugged. 'Their pool of general knowledge is pretty much limited to grass, milk and more grass.'

Bee laughed, in spite of the fact that she had vowed not to like Toby. 'Anything else you'd like to share?'

He grinned. 'Just one more. Your vagina is like a sheep's. Not yours specifically,' he added. 'Just the human vagina in general.'

Bee blinked again. *Vagina* was not the kind of word scruffy-haired boys usually used. But it was becoming clear that Toby was not an ordinary scruffy-haired boy. 'Does that line usually work for you?'

'Like you wouldn't believe.' He reached into his bag and pulled out a little silver flask. 'Drink?'

'No thanks.' Bee turned back to her possum.

'So what did your boyfriend want?' asked Toby after a few minutes.

'It wasn't my boyfriend.'

'But you do have a boyfriend, right?'

'Yes,' said Bee, although she wasn't entirely sure that was true. Fletch hadn't made contact with her all summer. It was possible that he'd gone away with his family, but surely a dutiful boyfriend would send a postcard, or at the very least a text message to say Happy New Year. Of course Bee hadn't contacted him either – she wasn't going to be anyone's pathetic nagging girlfriend. But the fact remained that she hadn't heard from him in nearly four weeks, and that didn't exactly bode well for the future (or even existence) of their relationship.

'You sure about that?'

'It's none of your business.'

'Hit a nerve, did I?' Toby smiled an infuriatingly knowing smile. 'Sorry. I'll drop it.'

He really was irritating. Of course he'd hit a nerve! But did he have to go and *talk* about it and *ask rude questions* instead of just shutting up like a normal, polite person would? She was at work; she didn't want to talk about her *feelings*.

A part of Bee quietly pointed out that she was more annoyed by a guy she'd only known for twelve hours than she was by her apparent rejection at the hands of actual real-life boyfriend. The thing was, Bee felt faintly relieved to have been dumped (if, in fact, she had been). Fletch was good-looking, and he never talked about uncomfortable stuff or made exasperatingly teasing eyes at her, but he wasn't very bright and he had a habit of picking his teeth in public. And while Bee had enjoyed the status that having a boyfriend like Fletch had bestowed upon her, he was a bit... *boring*. There was only so long a girl could sit around a guy's living room watching him play Mario Kart before the shine wore off. If she'd been the kind of person who was fascinated by the pounding of a Wii controller, she could have just stayed home and hung out with her mother. At least Angela played more interesting games.

Despite all that, nobody liked to be dumped, and Bee's pride was wounded. Fletch could at least have called her to let her know it was over. But she had a pretty good idea why he hadn't, although she was choosing not to think about it. In any case, Bee had no desire to share any of this with smarmy smirking Toby, who was taking a slug from the flask and studying her with his twinkly eyes behind their hipster glasses.

Seeing her glare, he proffered the flask again. Bee's glare intensified, and she shook her head.

Toby laughed. 'Up to you.'

Bee wondered what would happen if she took it. She didn't get the whole drinking thing; she couldn't really see the point. But right now, she figured there were three options.

1. Maintain her stoic refusal, finish her possum and leave as soon as possible.
2. Have one very small sip from the flask, just to get Toby off her back.
3. Have a somewhat larger sip from the flask, and see what happened.

Although Bee had most definitely decided on Option 1, she couldn't help being intrigued about the possibilities of Option 3, and felt it required a sub-list of potential outcomes.

a. The alcohol would make Bee relax, and Toby might seem less irritating. In fact, it might lead to other things. Fun things. Things that Bee hadn't associated with Toby before. Like touching that scruffy hair. Or seeing him without those trendy black glasses. Or sliding her hand behind the collar of that vintage penguin polo shirt... Stop!
b. It would make Bee drunk, and she would do something stupid and/or embarrassing that she would definitely regret.
c. She would become an alcoholic, her brain cells would instantly decay and she would forever rue the day she allowed herself to be tempted by peer pressure.

It was undeniably safest to go with Option 1. Stoic refusal was the only acceptable course of action. Bee was about to open her mouth and express this to Toby, but swallowed and coughed at the sudden burning feeling in the back of her throat. She swallowed again and realised with chagrin that while her brain had been busy calculating the pros and cons of accepting Toby's whisky, her body had simply gone ahead and done it without any consultation. She felt her cheeks redden, and handed the flask back to Toby. She wasn't a blusher! Who *was* this boy who could just waltz into her laboratory and turn her into an alcohol-consuming blusher?

Stoic refusal was clearly no longer an option.

Ⓘ Ⓘ Ⓘ

'Did you know,' said Toby, slurring slightly, 'that slugs have four noses?'

They were sitting on the floor. According to the clock on the wall, it was 12:06. Bee's head felt a little fuzzy.

'I did not know that,' she said. 'I don't like slugs. Snails are better.'

'They *are* better,' said Toby. 'They have teeth, too. One day I will tell you something beautiful and a little bit dirty about snails.'

'Tell me now!'

Toby shook his head. 'I don't think you're ready for it.'

'Fine. So what else do you know?'

'I know *so* many things. I know that the goldfish is the only animal in the whole world who can see in infrared and ultraviolet. I know that more people have been killed by fleas than by other people. I know that every mammal has seven vertebrae in their necks, even giraffes with their very long necks and rugby players with no necks at all. Except for manatees and two-toed sloths, which have six vertebrae. And three-toed sloths have *nine*, which seems greedy to me.'

'I don't understand,' said Bee, who was also struggling to comprehend simple concepts such as *talking* and *where her hands were supposed to go when she wasn't using them*.

'It's so they can turn their heads all the way around when they're hanging upside down,' explained Toby.

'No,' said Bee, shaking her head and making her entire world turn upside down for a moment. 'I understand about the sloths. Why do you *know* all those things?'

Toby squinted at the flask. 'Actually, the two-toed sloth has three toes,' he said. 'It has two *fingers*. It's not very closely related to the three-toed sloth, even though you can barely tell the difference by looking at them. Their common ancestor lived about forty million years

24

ago, making it a rather exquisite example of convergent evolution.'

This speech was delivered with knowledgeable flair, which Toby ruined completely by belching at the end.

Bee stared at him. 'This is how you try to impress girls, isn't it?'

'Maybe,' said Toby. 'Is it working?'

Bee shrugged. 'A little,' she admitted. 'But seriously. Why the internal encyclopaedia?'

Toby laughed. 'I want to be a Thingy. You know.'

'Quiz-show winner?'

'No.' Toby shook his head. 'A zoo—'

'Keeper?'

Toby smirked. '—ologist,' he said. 'A zoologist. Or an entomologist, I haven't decided yet.'

'But you're studying medicine,' said Bee.

Toby looked at her. 'Yes,' he said, nodding. 'Yes, I am. Not studying veterinary science at all. *Medicine.*'

'So is that why you're here? To do some of the zoology stuff?'

'Sure. Let's go with that.'

Bee was beginning to think that maybe if she hadn't drunk from the little silver flask, she wouldn't be so confused. 'Why *are* you here?'

25

Toby took another swig. 'I failed my final exam last year. That's the reason I'm here. To make up the extra credit.'

'Why did you fail?'

Toby looked away. 'What's through that door?' He waved the flask towards the low stone archway by Gus's desk.

Bee wondered in a blurry sort of way why Toby was being evasive. Was he embarrassed that he'd failed his exam? Or was it something else? More importantly, what did his hair smell like? It looked as though it would smell nice.

'The old Catacombs,' she said, trying to push away the thought of Toby's hair. 'About fifty years' worth of old stuffed animals and empty glass cases.'

'Sounds creepy.'

'It is. All those glass eyes and dust.'

'So let's go and check it out.' Toby stood up.

Bee shook her head. 'We should really get back to work.'

'Great idea,' said Toby, snorting. 'Because what you should do after drinking whisky is handle dangerous chemicals, knives and needles.'

'I'm not *drunk*,' said Bee. 'I'm *fine*. Plus we don't use dangerous chemicals anymore.'

She climbed to her feet and was somewhat concerned

to find they now seemed to be much further from her head than she was accustomed to.

'I feel like Alice,' she whispered, then giggled because her voice sounded funny. She noticed through the fuzziness that Gus had left his smartcard on his desk. How would he get into the building the next morning? He'd have to call Security.

'Come on,' said Toby, and grabbed her hand. His hand was warm, and bigger than hers. Bee let him pull her towards the wooden door, which he pushed open with his other hand, then guided her head down as they ducked through the archway.

'It's dark!' whispered Bee. 'How will we see? Did you bring a torch?'

'No,' said Toby. 'I brought my magic finger.'

'What? You don't have a magic...oh.'

Toby had flicked a switch, and a fluorescent light *plink-plink*ed on overhead.

It really did look like ancient catacombs. The ceilings were low and vaulted, creating individual alcoves separated by concrete columns. The chambers stretched in every direction as far as the fluorescent light reached, then they faded into darkness. Bee imagined that they just went on forever and ever.

Toby tried to stand up straight and bumped his head on the ceiling. 'Ow,' he said, and then, '*Cool.*'

They were standing among a herd of gazelles, all jumbled together with their horns tangled in the exposed electrical wiring looping from the ceiling, and their hooves crowded with cardboard boxes full of old brochures.

The light glinted off a hundred glass eyes. Bee realised that Toby was still holding her hand. She decided she liked it.

They picked their way through the gazelles, clambered over the back half of a rhinoceros, and found themselves in the African savannah. A baby hippo frolicked by a forest of plastic buckets and dirty mops. The light wasn't as strong here, and Bee couldn't see another light switch. It was as if they were on the edge of nothingness.

She thought she felt something brush against her calf and turned. She was face to face with a tiger, frozen mid-stride, teeth bared. Bee jumped and dropped Toby's hand, then scolded herself. It looked very real, despite the layer of dust and the fuzz of cottonwool poking out of its left ear.

'I think you should ride it,' said Toby with an evil grin.

'No!'

'Go on. I won't tell anyone.'

28

Bee couldn't believe she was behaving like this. But she was feeling warm and reckless after being startled by the tiger. Why not?

She gripped the tiger's neck and swung her leg over its back.

'What do you think?' she said, striking a pose.

Toby nodded. 'Hot,' he said. 'Very hot. Like a Persian goddess.'

Bee felt a flush creep up under her collar. She was a little tingly. She stroked the tiger's neck.

'That looks like fun,' said Toby. 'Do you reckon he's strong enough to take us both?'

'I think it's a she.'

'Even better.'

Bee held onto the tiger's ears as Toby climbed on behind her. His arms slid around her waist and his chest pressed against her back.

'So where should we go?' Toby's breath tickled in Bee's left ear.

Bee was vaguely aware of Toby's hands pressing against her belly. But most of her attention was on his lips, which lightly brushed her neck.

'Um,' she said. 'I'm not sure. Brazil? The Amazon? The Moon?'

'Brazil sounds good.'

Bee leaned her head back on his shoulder so he could kiss her cheek and jaw. He certainly seemed to know his way around better than Fletch.

'You know,' he said, his voice low, 'the only other species that kisses is the white-fronted parrot. They lock their beaks before mating and gently flick their tongues together. Of course the next step in their courtship is that the male regurgitates all over the female, so we don't have to follow their methods to the letter. But the first bit sounds like it could be fun…'

Little shivers of lightning ran up and down Bee's spine. She twisted around to face him so they could start kissing properly.

And then the light went out. Bee froze. Toby pulled away.

'Well, *that*'s never happened before,' he said.

She dug her fingernails into the tiger's fur. 'What did happen?' she whispered.

'I don't know. Come on.'

The door into the lab was still open, spilling warm yellow light into the darkness of the Catacombs. They clambered off the tiger and stumbled towards the light, barking their shins on bits of hyena and elephant, and stubbing their toes on low glass cases and concrete plinths.

As Bee brushed past the last gazelle, she saw a figure silhouetted in the doorway for a brief moment. Then the door swung shut and engulfed them in darkness.

Bee began to tremble. No. She was just being silly. It was probably a security guard, doing his nightly rounds. Or maybe Gus had returned to get his smartcard.

Footsteps sounded in the lab. Bee saw the thin strip of light beneath the door wink out, then the footsteps faded into the distance. Bee groped for Toby's hand, and they felt their way to the door, which had thankfully not been locked on the other side.

Toby flicked the lab light back on and Bee blinked away the brightness. She felt tired and fuzzy, as though her head was stuffed with tissue paper.

'You okay?' said Toby.

'Fine.' Her voice sounded as though it were a long way away. 'It was probably the security guard.'

'Yeah,' said Toby. He looked at her for a moment longer, and Bee thought maybe he was going to kiss her again. 'I might just go and check, though,' he said. 'Make sure he doesn't lock us in or set an alarm or anything.'

'Okay.'

Toby slipped out the door into the corridor. Bee shivered, suddenly cold. She perched on her desk. The almost-finished possum stared up at her with empty eye-sockets.

She felt as if she'd been busted breaking into school at night. But she hadn't. She'd been *working late*, which was something professional and responsible. Something adult. Adults worked late.

Adults didn't get hot and sticky with boys on the backs of stuffed tigers.

Bee checked the clock on the wall: 12:49. She'd have to get a cab home. Toby had been gone for eleven minutes. Why was she waiting? Was it because she thought she and Toby would resume their make-out session when he got back? She had a strong, urgent desire to be at home, in bed. Alone.

She picked up her bag just as Toby returned.

'No sign of the security guard,' said Toby. 'And his office is empty, so I guess he's on his rounds somewhere else in the building.' He looked at her. 'Are you leaving?'

'Um,' said Bee. 'Yeah. It's late.'

She shuffled awkwardly towards the door, veering to the side in case Toby thought she was walking towards *him*.

'See you tomorrow,' she said.

'Yeah,' said Toby. 'See you.'

3

BEE WOKE TO THE SOUNDS of her mother being attacked with a light sabre.

She crawled out of bed, every swoop and crack of the light sabre stabbing her between the eyes.

Angela was sitting on the couch in the living room, wearing a red velvet dressing-gown and battling Darth Vader on her PlayStation 3.

'Hi, Mum,' said Bee.

Angela didn't look away from the screen, but waved her controller in a vague gesture that Bee supposed was meant to be affectionate. 'Good morning, sweetheart.' She performed a tricky manoeuvre that involved jumping high in the air and flipping over before slamming Darth Vader on the top of his black shiny helmet. 'Did you go out last night? Did you have fun?'

Bee thought of the little silver flask, the stuffed tiger, and the feeling of Toby's lips on her neck.

'No,' she said. 'I had to work late, remember?'

'That's a shame.' Angela winced as she took a glancing blow to the head. 'So do you have the morning off? I'm nearly finished this chapter and I don't have to teach until 11:30. We could go out for breakfast.'

Bee shook her head. 'No,' she said, yawning. 'I still have to be there at the normal time.'

Darth Vader delivered a killing blow and the screen went dark. Angela swore and threw down her controller. Then she glanced up at Bee. 'Sweetheart, I'm sorry to break it to you, but normal time left the building a while ago.'

Bee felt as though she'd been slapped in the face. She looked at the clock on the DVR. It was 9:03.

'Crap,' she said, and bolted to her room to change.

ⓘ ⓘ ⓘ

Bee's perfectly honed skills of observation were sadly dulled by residual alcohol, lack of sleep and intruding thoughts about a certain dark-haired, bespectacled boy and the way he had sent shivers up her spine. So she didn't notice five things that otherwise would have alerted her to the fact that this Friday morning was not like other Friday mornings.

1. The front door of the museum didn't open automatically as it usually did within opening hours. Bee had to fish out her smartcard and buzz in.
2. An A3 piece of paper was stuck to the automatic door with sticky tape. Bee didn't stop to read what it said.
3. The museum café was closed.
4. Bee didn't have her watch on, so she didn't notice that, despite it being 10:17, there were no patrons lined up at the ticket counter.
5. There were no staff at the ticket counter. There were no staff anywhere.

Bee passed through the Mollusc Room and the Hall of Native Flora, then pressed her smartcard against a door and pushed it open, making her way down the grey concrete stairs to the basement.

Two police officers, a man and a woman, were standing at the bottom of the stairs, talking in low voices.

Bee walked up to them. 'Would you mind letting me through?' she said, as if a police presence outside her office wasn't at all unusual. 'I'm late.'

'Sorry,' said the policeman. 'But I'm afraid I can't do that.'

Bee sighed and was about to argue, but someone called her name. It was Toby.

'Are you okay?' he said, touching her arm. Bee pulled away, feeling affronted. Why wouldn't she be okay? What did she have to be not okay about? She considered it and came up with three possible scenarios, none of which were acceptable.

1. Toby was in love with her, and had immediately turned into the kind of boy who buys bunches of roses with those little white flowers among them. The kind of boy she'd read about who wrote *poetry* and was doglike and droopy. The kind of boy who said *no, you hang up first*. And Bee had no interest in that kind of boy, in fiction or in real life.

2. Toby was concerned that *she* was in love with *him*. And he was going to play the *man, we were so trashed last night, what the hell did we get up to* card to get himself out of trouble. Well.

3. Gus was on the warpath because Bee was late. Which would mean Bee getting a lecture from Gus, while Toby stood around in the background looking smarmy.

Whatever the reason behind Toby's solicitousness, Bee decided to clear up the whole drunken-kissing thing straight off.

'Look,' she said, glancing at the police officers and scowling. 'About last night. I think we're probably both mature enough to admit that things got a little out of hand. And while I'm sure you're a very nice person, I really don't think we have much in common. So perhaps we could just forget it ever happened. We have to work together, and...would you mind letting go of my arm?'

Toby did not let go of her arm. He tugged on it instead. 'We have to go upstairs, Bee.'

Bee wasn't sure how that was a mature response to her statement...or any response, really. Why did he want her to go upstairs? Did he want to find a private place so he could kiss her again? Was he not listening? She didn't want any more kissing. Really. Honestly. She felt her cheeks go red.

'There's a staff meeting,' Toby was saying. 'We've all been summoned.'

He was still pulling on her arm. The police officers were staring uncomfortably at the ground.

'What?' said Bee. 'There's no staff meeting today. Staff meetings are on Mondays.'

Toby stopped pulling, and leaned down to look Bee directly in the eye.

'Bee, don't you know?' he said. 'Gus is dead.'

4

'MOST OF YOU WILL ALREADY have heard that Gus, our Head Taxidermist, died last night,' said Akiko Kobayashi, the Museum Director, her knuckles white on the wooden lectern.

Bee sat next to Toby in the back row of the auditorium where the museum held public lectures and forums. The other staff members were dotted around the room, sitting in groups of two or three. Some were crying. Bee felt as if she couldn't blink. The only part of her body that had any feeling was the hand Toby was still holding. Gus was *dead*?

'Are you okay?' whispered Toby, squeezing her hand.

Bee didn't respond.

'He was found this morning in the Red Rotunda,' said Akiko, glancing down at a piece of paper in front of her. She paused and swallowed. 'The police say that he – he took his own life. At around midnight last night. He took something that sent him into anaphylactic shock. Um. Forensics are working in the Red Rotunda today, so please stay away from that area. Counselling will be made available to any staff member who requests it, and of course my door is always open. The museum will remain closed today, and staff have the option of taking the rest of the day off...'

Akiko continued to talk, but all Bee heard was a faint buzzing. Gus was dead. *Dead.* Yesterday he ate a salad sandwich and two hamburgers and several doughnuts and today he was dead. As dead as the possum on Bee's desk.

'I need to see him,' Bee said suddenly, turning to Toby.

'What?'

'Gus. I need to see him.'

'You want to see his body?'

Bee nodded. 'Now,' she said, getting to her feet.

There was police tape across the door of the Red Rotunda, but no sign of any officers.

'We can't go in,' said Toby.

Bee ignored him and opened the door, ducking under the tape.

The room looked the same as it had the previous day. It contained a strange collection of creatures, some preserved in jars of yellowing methylated spirits, others posed and mounted. There were some rather mangy cats and a dog in one case, and a scorpion and a funny-shaped crab in another. One large jar labelled MOLE PAWS contained what looked like several hundred tiny furry hands. A raven perched on a wooden branch, its glass eye winking at Bee.

The only change in the room was that the elderly gentleman and tour guide were gone, replaced by two police officers standing near a glass case containing a dissected dolphin fin and a sperm whale foetus.

And Gus, lying in the very middle of the room, not moving.

He was on his back, his green Natural History Museum hoodie stark against the polished parquetry floor and the red walls. His eyes were closed and his mouth open. In his right hand Bee saw a tiny bottle. She leaned forward to read the label.

'Seriously?' said one of the policemen into a mobile phone. He held the phone to his chest to muffle his voice as he spoke to his colleague. 'Forensics can't get back here until two.'

'The guy's been dead for…' The second policeman checked his watch. '…nearly eleven hours. He's going to start to smell.'

Bee went to check the time, only to find her watch wasn't on her wrist. She grabbed Toby's arm. There was an awkward moment where he seemed to think Bee wanted to hold his hand, but she pulled back his sleeve impatiently and checked his watch: 10:51.

The movement caught the attention of the policeman on the phone, who frowned at them. 'I don't care if it's only routine, just tell them to hurry.' He finished the call. 'You can't be in here,' he said to Bee and Toby.

'Sorry,' said Toby. 'We work here. In the same office as...' He indicated Gus and glanced at Bee. 'My colleague is very upset.'

The policeman nodded. 'It must be hard,' he said. 'And ordinarily it'd be fine, but Forensics haven't finished yet, and I'll be in deep strife if I let anyone near the body.'

'Does he have anything on him?' asked Bee suddenly. Her voice sounded very loud.

'I'm sorry?'

'Besides the bottle. Does he have his wallet, or a suicide note, or anything?'

The policeman shook his head. 'Nothing,' he said. 'Just some loose change in the pocket of his hoodie. Oh, and about ten glass eyes.'

'What size?' asked Bee. Toby looked at her as if she were crazy.

'Different sizes,' said the policeman. 'Like for an animal. Yellow, with a line instead of a dot in the middle.'

'Like a cat's eye?' asked Bee.

42

'More like a lizard or a snake's.' The policeman made an apologetic face. 'You'd better go. There's really not supposed to be anyone in here.'

Toby escorted Bee out the front door of the museum and across the lawn to the posh café over the road. As they walked, Bee's mind was whirling. But amid the confusion of emotions and thoughts, three things stood out very clearly:

1. It was a very nice day. Too nice to be the day you discover your boss has killed himself.
2. The old man she'd seen yesterday – William Cranston – was sitting on a bench on the museum lawn. He was wearing a tweed cap.
3. Bee was a terrible, terrible person.

In the café, Toby bought her a cup of chamomile tea and an orange-cardamom friand.

'You're sure you're okay?' he asked.

'Yeah,' she said. 'Sorry about before. I was upset.'

'I know. I'm upset too. It's...it sucks.'

Bee shook her head. 'I just don't understand.'

'Me neither,' said Toby. 'I mean, I barely knew the guy, but why would *Gus* want to kill himself? He must have been really unhappy.'

'He didn't *seem* unhappy,' said Bee. 'Grumpy, but not unhappy. And yesterday he was positively chirpy.'

'It's common for behaviour to alter dramatically once the decision has been made to end a life,' said Toby, as if he were reciting from a book. Bee frowned at him and he looked apologetic. 'But you're right, it's weird.'

'Yeah,' said Bee, staring into her cup of tea while her mind clicked and whirred through myriad possibilities and scenarios, none of which involved a suicide. 'Weird.'

Stop. She had to stop thinking like a storybook detective. This was real life. A man was *dead*. 'Have you heard of William Cranston?' she asked suddenly. 'He's an anatomist.'

Toby looked confused. 'Um, I don't know. The name sounds familiar. Are you sure you're okay?'

'Yes,' said Bee firmly. 'I'm fine. Gus killed himself. It's very sad and real. I'm fine.'

Toby leaned closer. 'You sound like you're trying to convince yourself. You don't think he killed himself?'

Bee forced a laugh. 'Of course he did. That's what the policeman said.'

'But you think they might be wrong? What, do you think he might have been *murdered*?'

'No,' said Bee. 'No. Definitely not.'

44

She just had to stop thinking, that was all. Maybe if Toby kissed her neck again it would drive out all rational thought like last time.

'Because, really, why would anyone want to kill Gus? I'm sure he didn't have any money or anything.'

'Exactly,' said Bee. 'It can't have been murder.'

Toby ducked his head to look directly at her. 'You don't look convinced,' he observed.

Bee stood up suddenly, her chair scraping on the slate tiles. 'Well, I am,' she said shortly. 'I'm going home.'

'Wait,' said Toby, but Bee was already marching out of the café and into the bright sunshine.

The whole idea seemed even more ridiculous in the street, with people walking by eating ice-cream and carrying shopping bags. But there were so many things sloshing around in Bee's head, getting tangled up in her hangover and making her temples throb. She closed her eyes for a moment and wondered how it was possible that Toby knew so much random trivia about the anatomy of creatures, but had never heard of Doctor William Cranston. Shouldn't a trivia-laden med student like Toby be familiar with a world-famous anatomy expert?

'Bee,' said Toby. 'Talk to me. What's going on?'

He touched her shoulder and she had a sudden flash-back to the stuffed tiger and the little silver flask. They hadn't talked about what had happened last night. Bee hoped that now they wouldn't have to. She also remembered seeing Gus's smartcard on his desk after she was introduced to the little silver flask. She remembered hearing the door to the taxidermy lab close. She remembered going back into the lab and noticing the three-minutes-slow clock, which had read 12:38. Had the smartcard still been on Gus's desk when they returned? That she couldn't remember. Stupid silver flask.

'Bee?'

'Nothing,' said Bee, who had an uncomfortable suspicion that she might cry from the enormity of it all, and the nagging thoughts and emerging theories that she couldn't drive away. 'Nothing is going on. Because I *know* Gus wasn't murdered. I know because the world doesn't work that way. Have you heard of Occam's razor?'

Toby made a face. 'It's one of those things I always pretend to know about when lecturers mention it,' he admitted. 'But I've got no idea.'

'It's this scientific theory,' said Bee, talking very quickly to stop herself from bursting into tears, 'that the simplest explanation is usually the right one. And it *is*. My father didn't disappear when I was six because he got stranded on a desert island like Robinson Crusoe. He left because he was embarrassed by my mother, who

46

is a spotty sixteen-year-old comic-book nerd living in the rather overweight body of a middle-aged woman. And my boyfriend Fletch hasn't called me all summer – not because he's a secret agent on a mission in Russia, but because he likes my best friend better than he likes me.' She took a deep breath. 'The world isn't complicated at all. It's very simple and straightforward. Mysteries can be solved with clear, objective thinking. Gus killed himself because he was depressed. There. The end.'

'But?' said Toby.

'But what?'

'Oh, there's a *but*. I know you have a *but*. So tell me. *But...*?'

Bee stared at him for a moment. She should just keep quiet. *But...*

'But yesterday, Gus didn't seem like the kind of man who was so depressed he was about to kill himself. He told us all that bizarre stuff about Frankenstinian dogs. He ate a *sandwich*. And that bottle...the label said it was corrosive sublimate. I'm not quite sure what that is. But anyway, it was in his *right* hand, yet Gus was *left*-handed. And how did he get into the Red Rotunda if he'd left his smartcard in the office?'

'Maybe he had a key?'

'But you need a smartcard to get into the public galleries out of hours. And the policeman said he'd been dead for eleven hours, which puts his time of death at around midnight. So who did we hear in our office at 12:38? Was it Gus? Who else was around? And what was with his pocketful of glass eyes?'

'Wow.' Toby took a half-step back from her. 'You really don't think he killed himself, do you?'

Bee shook her head. 'No, I really don't. There's something else, too, but I can't quite figure it out.' She put her hand to her forehead. 'I need to get some sleep.'

'I'll help you,' said Toby.

'No thanks. I've been managing to fall asleep solo since I was eighteen months old.'

'I mean, I'll help you get to the bottom of the Gus thing,' said Toby. 'I'll be the Watson to your Holmes. Your sidekick.'

Bee swallowed. 'I think we should go to the police.'

5

BEE PRESSED THE RED 'HANG UP' button on her phone and slipped it back into her bag with a sigh.

'No luck?' said Toby. They were sitting on the museum lawn.

'The detective I spoke to said they'd look into it,' she said. 'But he didn't sound very interested. He said they didn't routinely investigate suicides.'

'So it's up to us.'

Bee shook her head. 'This is serious stuff. A guy is dead.'

This was what she had spent her whole life wishing for: a real mystery, with clues and suspicious circumstances, and the police refusing to get involved. It was all there, waiting for her. But she should walk away. The police would figure it out.

'Okay, fine,' said Toby. 'But what would you do next, just for argument's sake?'

'What?'

'If it *wasn't* real life. If you *were* Nancy Drew or Sherlock Holmes or whoever. WWPD?'

'WWPD?'

'What Would Poirot Do?'

Bee knew he was trying to trick her into getting involved. She should ignore him. Change the subject. Go home. But it was already there, in her mind. It couldn't hurt to...

'I'll only tell you if you promise not to do *anything*,' she said. 'You cannot get involved.'

Toby traced an *X* on his chest with one finger. 'I promise.'

'Okay.' Bee pondered for a moment. 'The first step I'd take would be to find out more about Gus. I don't think he'd been working at the museum for very long – what did he do before that? Did he have a family? Where did he live? Either there's a reason why he killed himself, or there's a motive for someone else to have murdered him. Getting a picture of who he was – what kind of a person, his likes and dislikes, his history – might help figure out what happened.'

'Then what?'

'Well, if suicide still wasn't looking likely, I'd make a list of everyone who might benefit from his death. It'd help if we could get hold of his will.'

Toby nodded. 'And then investigate each suspect? Interview them and check their alibis?'

'More or less.' Bee shot him a pointed look. 'But you aren't going to *do* any of that, are you?'

Toby's eyes were wide. 'Bee,' he said. 'I *promised*. I never go back on a promise.'

◑ ◑ ◑

Angela was in the shower when Bee arrived home. Bee flopped onto the couch and turned on the TV, but couldn't pay any attention to whichever celebrity was getting a makeover.

In her brain, two Guses kept flashing before her eyes. One Gus was eating a sandwich with beetroot dangling from it. The other Gus was grey and cold on the floor of the Red Rotunda.

It just didn't make sense.

Bee's mum emerged from her bedroom with wet hair, wearing a floor-length purple velvet dress and a green cape.

'You're home early,' she said. 'Have you seen my amulet?'

Bee pointed to the bookshelf. Angela retrieved a silver pendant with a purple crystal in the centre surrounded by runes, and fastened it around her neck.

'I've got D&D tonight,' she said, 'so you'll have to get your own dinner. There's some leftover Chinese in the fridge, or a few single-white-lady meals in the freezer.'

Bee nodded.

'Bee?' said Angela. 'Are you okay?'

Bee swallowed. 'I've always liked mystery stories, right?'

'Since birth.' Angela chuckled. 'All I wanted was to read you *The Hobbit*, but you weren't interested in anything that didn't involve a detective and a dead body.'

'Did you think it was weird?'

Angela gave her a flat look. 'Darling-heart, in about ten minutes I'm going to strap on a sword and sit around a table with my friends rolling dice and pretending to kill monsters with the aid of an imaginary Celestial Badger called Gavin. And you're asking if I think you liking crime fiction is weird?'

'Good point.'

'What's all this about? You look upset.'

'Something happened today,' said Bee. 'My supervisor at work killed himself.'

Angela sat down and gave Bee a hug. 'Darling,' she said. 'Are you okay?'

'I'm not sure. I keep trying to be sad and act like a normal person. But I can't help thinking that if this was a mystery novel, he wouldn't have killed himself. He would have been murdered. And then I think about how and why, and…and it isn't *normal*.'

Angela's amulet poked into Bee's chest. 'Bee,' she said. 'There's no right or wrong way to deal with death. You deal with it however is best for you.'

'But it's *dangerous*!' said Bee. 'And statistically, he probably did kill himself. Do you know suicide is the eleventh-highest cause of death in the United States? Suicide outnumbers *homicide* by two to one, and not all homicides are murders. So the chances of him being murdered are pretty slim.'

Angela raised her eyebrows. 'Okay, the fact that you can just pull those statistics up *is* weird. What are they teaching you at school?'

Bee scowled. 'Can I talk to the Celestial Badger? I think he might be more helpful.'

Angela gave her a squeeze. 'I hear what you're saying. The world is scary. Why do you think I spend so much time living in a world where there are good elves and evil trolls, where you can tell a person's allegiance by what colour light sabre they carry?'

'I thought you just did it because you're a dork.'

Angela punched Bee lightly. 'None of your cheek, missy.'

Bee stared at the television for a moment.

'Mum?'

'Yes, sweetheart?'

'I think I'm more frightened by the idea that Gus killed himself than by the idea of him being murdered. Is there something wrong with me?'

'Not at all,' said Angela, smoothing Bee's hair. 'There is nothing in any way wrong with you. It's terrifying to think someone could be so unhappy that they don't want to live anymore.'

Bee nodded.

'Now,' said Angela, 'do you want me to cancel tonight? I can stay home and we can watch that episode of *Star Trek* where Picard turns into a hard-boiled gumshoe on the holodeck.'

'I'll be fine,' said Bee. 'I'm just going to have a bath and go to bed.'

'You're sure?'

'I wouldn't want Gavin to have to go it alone. He might get his whiskers bent.'

Bee's mum kissed her forehead, then stood up and slung her backpack over her shoulder. 'Well, call me if you need anything – I'll keep my phone on,' she said, whacking her sword on the doorframe as she waved goodbye.

Bee turned her attention back to the television.

At 8:55 PM, she got the cold beef in black bean sauce and Singapore noodles out of the fridge and took it back to the couch without bothering to heat it up.

At 9:02 the evening newsbreak came on. Bee stopped eating and steeled herself, in case there was a mention of Gus's death. There wasn't. Just some stuff about a government cabinet meeting, and an attempted burglary of some mansion in Healesville.

At 9:12, Bee's phone rang. She checked the caller ID: her best friend Maddy. For an instant she considered answering – she could have used someone to talk to about Gus's death. And about the incident with the little silver flask and Toby and the tiger. But Bee didn't answer, because she was pretty sure that instead of talking about Toby and the tiger and Gus, Maddy would want to talk about why she hadn't called Bee all summer. And Bee was also sure that the reason Maddy hadn't called her all summer had something to do with Bee's boyfriend Fletch.

Who, now that Bee thought about it, wasn't really her boyfriend anymore.

Bee turned off her phone and wondered if there was any ice-cream in the freezer.

◍ ◍ ◍

Bee spent the weekend doing decidedly unmysterious things. She watched TV, ate pasta, read one of her set English texts for Year Twelve, and played Star Wars Trivial Pursuit with her mother. Angela seemed somehow distracted, checking her phone regularly, and forgetting the difference between a bantha and a tauntaun.

'Are you okay?' asked Bee.

'Hmm?' said Angela, looking up from her phone. 'Sorry, I'm fine. Is it my turn to ask a question?'

Bee didn't press her any further. She wasn't interested in mysteries.

① ① ①

On Monday morning, everything seemed to have returned to normal. Bee swiped her smartcard at the museum's front door, and then made her way down through the labyrinth of corridors and stairs to the Catacombs. Pushing open the door of the taxidermy lab, she saw Adrian Featherstone, the Head Conservator, sitting at Gus's desk and rolling something between his thumb and forefinger.

There was an ongoing rivalry between the Preparators and the Conservators. The Preparators worked in the old-fashioned part of the building, surrounded by mess and chaos. In addition to the taxidermy lab, there were the maceration and freeze-drying labs, as well as a carpentry studio and the fabrication studio, where creatures were modelled in clay, moulded in silicone and then cast in polyurethane before being painted to look as real as possible. Every wall was covered in photos and posters and every shelf was crammed with skulls, stuffed penguins, dinosaur bones and strange things in jars. The Preparators themselves were mostly scruffy, jeans-wearing men in their thirties and forties.

The Conservation studio was a violent contrast. Located in the modern wing of the museum, the studio felt like an aircraft hangar, all white walls, fluorescent lighting and stainless steel benches. There was not a single book, folder or sheet of paper to be seen. Giant racks of bubble wrap, paper and muslin stood against one wall, and every other space was blindingly spotless. Bee thought it was like being in a hospital, a feeling which was only heightened by the fact that all the conservators seemed to be rather severe-looking pregnant women.

Except for the Head Conservator, Adrian Featherstone, a thin, weasel-faced man with a sulky mouth and a plummy British accent. He dressed like a once-rich homeless person, usually in a bizarre combination of dress slacks and a green museum hoodie, unzipped to reveal a stained T-shirt underneath. Everything about him seemed to be somehow out of control – his temper, his unbrushed, shoulder-length hair, his sloppy clothes. He always looked uncomfortable, and treated every other employee of the museum – even Museum Director Akiko Kobayashi – with extreme condescension. That condescension was now focused on Bee.

She jumped when she saw the eye in his hand. It was around a size 4, she thought, yellowish green with a strange-shaped pupil, like an eye for a lizard. Adrian Featherstone frowned, slipping the eye into his pocket.

'You're one of the casuals who was working with Gus, yes?' he asked.

'I'm Bee. I'm just here over the summer to help with the Fauna exhibit.'

Featherstone nodded briskly. 'Good. Obviously Gus will no longer be able to supervise you, and the Head Preparator is up to his waist in beached dead whale on the south coast.' He made a disgusted face. 'He won't be back for at least a week, so the preparation work will now have to be overseen by me. However, I'm sure you'll understand that I've plenty of other work on my plate, and won't have time to hold your hand. I trust that Gus taught you enough to work independently.'

Bee nodded.

'The exhibition plans are here.' Featherstone indicated the red lever-arch folder that had always sat on Gus's desk. 'I'll check on your progress when I can. If there are any problems you might be able to find me in my office; otherwise, my assistant will know where I am. And could you communicate all of this to your colleague, when he graces us with his presence?'

Bee nodded again, and Featherstone stood and left the room, an unpleasant odour of expensive aftershave and rotten apples lingering behind him.

Bee sat at her desk and picked up her watch from where she'd left it on Thursday night. She strapped it on her wrist, observing three things:

1. The clock on the wall seemed to have been fixed, as it was now showing the same time as her watch: 8:58 AM.

2. Gus's smartcard wasn't on his desk, although Bee supposed anyone could have removed it the previous day.

3. Bee did not like Adrian Featherstone one bit.

At 9:22, Bee's phone rang. It was her mother.

'I just wanted to check on you,' she said. 'Back at work, after...'

'I'm fine,' said Bee, still wondering exactly what it was about Adrian Featherstone that made her skin crawl.

'Good, because I've got something to tell you. Remember how I went to D&D on Friday night?'

'Yep,' said Bee, tracing her finger along the edge of the desk. Was it just the greasy hair and general grottiness of him? Or was there something else?

'Well, the most incredible thing happened, and I wanted to tell you over the weekend, but I wanted to be sure.'

'Really?' Bee hadn't really ever spoken to Featherstone before. She'd always dealt directly with Gus. He'd spoken a few times at staff meetings about the upcoming Flora and Fauna exhibition, but his monotonous English accent had made Bee zone out.

'Gavin assumed corporeal form!'

'What?' Bee wondered how long Featherstone had worked at the museum. She remembered one of the tour guides mentioning he hadn't lived in Australia long. And that he used to do something else. Not conservation.

'Gavin! We were on this mission that involved hunting down a band of Black Warlocks. And one of them cast a spell that turned Gavin into a human!'

'So Gavin's not a Celestial Badger anymore?' Gus hadn't liked Featherstone either. He'd once referred to him as a 'poncy weasel bastard'.

'No, he's a real live human who's now joined our party. Except his name is Neal, not Gavin.'

In fact, Bee had never seen Featherstone in the taxidermy lab before. She couldn't remember ever having seen Gus and Featherstone speak to each other. And Gus had refused to attend staff meetings.

'Anyway,' said her mother. 'We kind of...hit it off. And he called me this morning to ask if I'd like to have dinner with him tonight, after I finish teaching.'

'Great,' said Bee.

'So I'm afraid you'll have to fend for yourself again. I'll leave you some money for pizza.'

'Okay,' said Bee absently. 'Wait, what? Gavin the Celestial Badger is taking you out to dinner?'

But Angela had already hung up.

By the time Toby arrived at 9:47 AM, Bee had nearly finished her possum, and was sewing up the skin around the neck with tiny neat stitches the way Gus had shown her.

'I have to talk to you,' said Toby. He sat on his swivel-chair and rolled it across the floor until it bumped against Bee's.

'The Head Conservator is supervising us now,' she told him.

'Adrian Featherstone?' asked Toby, frowning slightly. 'Have you met him?'

'Not properly, but I know who he is.'

Toby looked as though he was going to say something else, but didn't.

'We have to finish the taxidermy stuff ourselves,' said Bee. 'It shouldn't be too hard, though – there's only about another six animals to be done. Also, I think my mother is dating a badger.'

'Bee,' said Toby, slowly. 'I have to tell you something, but you have to promise not to get mad.'

Bee put down her needle and thread. 'What have you done?'

'Wait, did you say your mother is dating a badger?' said Toby. 'Is that young-people slang for something weird and deviant?'

'No,' said Bee. 'A real badger. Or a Celestial Badger, although to be honest I'm not quite sure what that means. But what did you do?'

'Is that even legal?'

'What did you *do*?'

'I went into Akiko Kobayashi's office, and I told her I needed to talk to someone about Gus.' Toby looked proud. 'I put on quite a performance, with real tears and everything. And when she got up to get me a glass of water, I stole this.'

62

He laid a manila folder on Bee's desk. 'It's Gus's human-resources file.'

'You *promised*,' Bee said, dismayed. 'You *promised* you wouldn't get involved!'

He held up a hand. 'Remember, *you* promised not to get mad.'

'I didn't promise anything.'

Toby grinned. 'Come on, you're a little bit impressed, aren't you? Aren't you?'

She was, a little. But she wasn't going to tell him that.

'Well?' he said. 'Don't you want to know what's inside?'

'No.'

'Really? Are you sure about that?'

'Yes, I'm sure. I don't want to know.'

'Come on,' said Toby with a sly look. 'I know your type. You wanted to be Nancy Drew when you were little, didn't you?'

Bee said nothing.

'Didn't you?'

'No,' said Bee. 'I hate Nancy Drew. She's too perfect. She's all prim and pretty and can cook and sew. *And* she can fly a plane and change a tyre and fix a flawed distributor.'

Toby raised his eyebrows. 'That's quite a list of achievements,' he said. 'I don't even know what a distributor is. Let alone how to tell if one is flawed.'

'I wanted to be Trixie Belden,' admitted Bee.

'Who?'

'Another girl detective. She lived in upstate New York and had adventures with horses and missing diamonds. She had a club with her friends and she hated doing chores and she was bad at maths and she didn't like her curly hair.'

Toby grinned. 'Well, this is your chance to be Trixie Belden. Take on the case, Bee.'

Bee scowled at him and turned back to her possum. She didn't want to be Trixie Belden. Trixie Belden was for little kids. If she were going to be any detective, she'd be Stephanie Plum from the Janet Evanovich books. Someone adult and sophisticated. Definitely not Trixie Belden.

She didn't want to be a detective at all.

Really.

Bee counted silently to herself, closing her eyes and breathing deeply. When she got to forty, she opened her eyes and turned around. Toby was still there, his chair up against hers, the manila folder in his hand.

'Fine,' she said crossly. 'Give it to me.'

He chuckled as he handed it over. Bee opened the folder. There were copies of Gus's payslips, his contract, dated five months previously, and a photocopied CV. She examined the CV. It was very short – a single page listing one previous employer, Nathan Brothers Funerary Services. Bee turned the paper over, looking for something else. Surely Gus must have worked as a taxidermist before? At other museums?

'What do you think?' asked Toby.

Bee didn't reply. She read the CV again.

'Bee?'

'I didn't know his surname,' she said. 'We worked together for nearly five months and I didn't know his surname.'

Toby didn't say anything, just put a warm hand on Bee's shoulder and squeezed.

'There's no address,' said Bee. 'Nowhere in this file is there an address. Just a mobile number.'

Toby took his hand off Bee's shoulder and dug in his pocket for his phone. 'Read it out,' he said.

Bee did so, and Toby punched in the number and held the phone to his ear. He listened for a moment, then hung up and put it back in his pocket.

'Generic voicemail.'

Bee leaned across her desk and switched on her PC. She hadn't used it much since she'd been working at the museum – just occasionally to google something or look up pictures of animals to check the width of their cheeks or the angle of their hind legs. When she had logged in and her desktop had appeared, she opened Firefox and went to the online phone directory. There was no record of Nathan Brothers Funerary Services. Bee tried *G Whittaker*, and got thirty-two results in Victoria.

'Wait,' said Toby, looking over her shoulder. 'You should search for A Whittaker. Surely Gus is short for Angus.'

'We'll try both,' Bee said, tapping at the keyboard and pulling up a second list. She hit Print.

The printer whirred and hummed. Toby turned to Bee. 'I did a good detectiving, huh?' he said. 'Stealing the file?'

'Not bad,' said Bee, grudgingly. 'But you're no Watson.'

'Oh, come on! I *cried* in front of Kobayashi. Surely that makes me a *little* bit Watsony.'

Bee shot him a sidelong glance. 'You know how I told you about Occam's razor?'

Toby nodded.

'It's named after a medieval friar called William of Ockham. He went to Oxford University but never finished his degree, and people called him *Venerabilis Inceptor*. That's what I'm calling you, until you earn your Watson stripes.'

'Venerable Interceptor?'

'Vener*abilis* In*cep*tor. It means Worthy Beginner.'

Toby laughed. 'You and I should join some kind of random trivia club.'

Bee pulled the two lists from the printer tray. She kept the list of G Whittakers and passed the A Whittakers to Toby. 'Call them tonight,' she said. 'We have to know more about Gus.'

Toby took the list with one hand, put the other on her knee and leaned in to look carefully at her, his eyes very blue behind his black-framed glasses. 'Seriously? You want to do this?'

Bee took a deep breath. Toby seemed to feel very comfortable about putting his hands on her. Bee wanted to be aloof and brush his hand away, but found that she couldn't quite manage it. 'Yes,' she said. 'I want to do this.'

She wasn't sure if she was talking about investigating Gus's death, or something else.

6

'HELLO?' SAID A WOMAN'S VOICE on the other end of the phone.

'Hi,' said Bee. 'This may sound like a strange question, but do you have an elderly relative called Gus?'

There was a pause. 'Gus? No. I have a son called Gary. Who is this? What are you selling?'

'Sorry to bother you,' said Bee. 'Thanks.'

She hung up and crossed the thirty-second name off the list. Her mobile pinged.

```
No luck. -Toby
```

Maybe Gus was from interstate? Maybe he didn't have any family. Or maybe he had changed his name. Or used a fake one.

Bee heard footsteps on the porch and looked up, expecting to see her mother come in the front door. But she didn't. There were voices outside, low voices, and the occasional laugh from Angela.

Bee wondered what a Celestial Badger looked like once it had taken on human form.

The talking stopped, and Bee couldn't hear anything. She pulled a face. Was her mother *making out with the Badger*? What if she invited him in? Bee hurried into her bedroom, closing the door and climbing into bed without brushing her teeth.

She listened carefully as the front door opened and closed, but she didn't hear any more voices, and only one set of footsteps walked into Angela's bedroom. Bee breathed a sigh of relief.

ⓘ ⓘ ⓘ

Toby was late again on Tuesday morning. Bee had a lizard propped up on a series of blocks as she carefully inserted pins in its face to keep its eyes open and its mouth in the correct shape for freeze-drying. The lizard looked like an acupuncture patient.

Bee contemplated Gus's empty desk. How could a man just disappear? It was as if he had never existed, and only her memory and a one-page CV were left.

Or were they?

Bee pushed her chair away from her desk and rolled over to Gus's. His desk may have been cleared, but Bee couldn't believe she hadn't looked in his drawer. She pulled it open, her heart thumping.

The drawer contained the following:

- Two scalpels, sizes 3 and 4
- Six scalpel blades, sizes 10–22
- Scissors, both bull-nosed and fine-pointed
- Fine-pointed forceps
- Electrical-wire cutters
- A box containing various needles, curved and straight
- Dressmaking pins
- Assorted balls of string, cotton and fishing wire
- A yellow canvas tape measure
- Metal wire of varying thicknesses
- A white chinagraph pencil
- A small box of nails
- Bead glue
- A lump of paraffin wax
- A box of acrylic paints
- Three small paintbrushes, tied together with a rubber band.

Bee sighed. Nothing even remotely clue-like.

'What exactly are you hoping to find in there?'

Bee jumped. Adrian Featherstone was standing in the doorway to the taxidermy lab, his eyes slitted in suspicion.

'Scissors,' said Bee, swallowing. 'Mine are blunt.'

Adrian Featherstone didn't reply, and Bee realised he must have already gone through Gus's drawer before she'd seen him yesterday. But why? What had he been looking for? Had he found it? Did he think that Gus had been murdered as well?

Adrian peered at her face as if he were looking for something. 'You didn't notice anything...out of the ordinary, did you? Before Gus died?'

Bee shook her head. Actually, there were a number of things she had noticed that were out of the ordinary, but she wasn't inclined to share them with Adrian Featherstone. He was the most suspicious thing she had encountered yet.

'Gus was a good friend of mine,' Adrian Featherstone said, taking a step towards Bee. 'A very good friend. I simply don't believe he would kill himself. So if there's anything you noticed that you think would help shed light on his death...'

Bee's eyes widened. 'You think someone killed him?'

'No, no,' said Featherstone, looking suddenly uncomfortable. 'No need to be so melodramatic. I just wish I

71

could understand *why* he did it. Did he ever mention anyone to you? Any friends or family?'

'He never mentioned *you*,' said Bee blandly. 'Shouldn't you know about his friends and family? Given that he was such a *very good friend*?'

Adrian Featherstone looked as if he wanted to shake her. Something was going on here. Bee was about to press him further when Toby arrived, apologising loudly for his lateness. He grinned at Featherstone.

'Hi Adrian,' he said, affecting a matesy drawl. 'It *is* Adrian, right? I'm Toby.'

Adrian Featherstone regarded him with cold eyes. 'I'm off to a board meeting,' he said to Bee. 'If you have any questions, or if there's something you'd like to talk about,' – he paused rather tackily for effect – 'I'll be back after lunch.'

He left the room.

'Is *he* on the list?' asked Toby. 'Because that man is the very definition of the word *suspect*.'

Bee nodded. 'Yeah,' she said. 'He's on the list. I think we need to poke around his office a bit.'

They waited until midmorning, when Bee was sure Adrian Featherstone would be in his board meeting. Then they made their way over to the Conservation Department, where they were stopped by a pregnant conservator with very straight blonde hair and a cold smile.

'He's not here,' she said. 'Can I help you with anything?' Her tone suggested that it was unlikely.

'There's a folder we need to collect from Adrian's office,' said Toby with a smile. 'He said he'd leave it on his desk for us.'

The conservator raised her eyebrows. 'He didn't say anything to me about—'

'We'll only be a minute,' said Toby. 'By the way, I really like that blouse.'

The conservator gave him a flat, unimpressed look, but waved them towards one of the offices. 'Good luck finding anything in there,' she said disapprovingly as she went to the handwashing station.

The office was small and very untidy in comparison with the rest of Conservation. Books and folders and papers were piled against every wall, and Bee could barely distinguish the desk. She appraised the room, noticing:

- Three apple cores, in various stages of decomposition
- One dead cockroach
- Five used coffee cups, two of them containing unpleasant mould specimens

- One green Natural History Museum hoodie, tangled in the wheels of Featherstone's desk chair
- A small pile of nail clippings on the edge of the desk
- A bottle of cheap whisky, badly hidden on top of the bookshelf
- A book entitled *Secret Weapons: Defenses of Insects, Spiders, Scorpions and Other Many-Legged Creatures* with seven watermelon-coloured Post-its stuck in between various pages.

'Wow,' said Toby. 'It's like a homeless person lives here. Without the smell of stale urine.'

Bee spotted a crumpled bath towel in a corner. 'It looks like he sleeps here sometimes,' she said.

'Hmm,' said Toby. 'I don't need a spider sense to figure out that this guy is as dodgy as hell. So what are we looking for?'

'I don't know,' said Bee. 'Anything that gives us clues about him or what his connection was to Gus.'

She gazed around the room, feeling a little over-whelmed. What *was* she looking for?

Toby nodded towards a framed case of butterflies on the wall.

'Look,' he said. 'A Monarch. These little guys fly over six thousand kilometres in a year – from Canada down to the Gulf of Mexico and back again.'

'Fascinating.' Bee rifled through the contents of Adrian Featherstone's desk drawers, then turned her attention to his in-tray.

'It *is* fascinating,' Toby said, pressing a finger against the case. 'My grandfather used to collect butterflies. They're always chasing the warm weather. They can't fly if their body temperature is less than thirty degrees Celsius. That's why the butterfly house at the zoo is so warm.'

Bee sighed. She'd found nothing. She went to examine the pinboard on the wall.

'Did you know that butterflies taste with their hind feet? Incredible creatures.'

Bee moved closer to the pinboard, then removed a small square of newspaper.

'Bee?'

Bee ran her eyes over the cutting, her heart hammering. She felt as though every single hair on her body was standing erect.

'Bee?' Toby touched her arm, making her head snap around.

'We have to get out of here,' she said. 'Something very strange is going on.'

Before Toby could object, she grabbed his hand and dragged him out of Adrian Featherstone's office.

'Did you find it?' asked the conservator.

'Um,' said Bee. 'No.'

'Perhaps we should call his mobile,' said the conservator, reaching for a phone.

'No, no, that's fine,' said Bee. 'I don't want to interrupt his meeting. I'll talk to him tomorrow.'

Back in the Catacombs, Bee took the scrap of newspaper out of her pocket.

'So what's the big find?' asked Toby, peering over her shoulder.

Bee smoothed the paper. It was a short article accompanied by a black-and-white photo, clipped neatly from a newspaper. The photo was of two men, standing side by side near a tree. The man on the right held a shotgun, and the other carried three dead rabbits tied together by the back legs. The man with the gun was grinning, and the other, taller man was looking away from the camera, down at the ground. Although the paper looked quite new, the photo had clearly been taken a long time ago – at least thirty years, judging by the clothes and haircuts.

'Is that…?' Toby leaned forward.

Bee nodded and pointed to the caption.

Scientist and Museum Benefactor William Cranston with his assistant, Gregory Uriel Swindon.

The taller man was unmistakably a young Gus.

Toby whistled. 'Gregory Uriel Swindon. Gus. But who's the other guy?'

Bee's hands were trembling. 'William Cranston. I asked you about him on Friday. He sponsored the Red Rotunda. I saw him in there on the morning before Gus...'

William Cranston's pale eyes sparkled in the photo. Even in black and white, she recognised those eyes. Although they hadn't been sparkling when she'd seen him in the Red Rotunda.

'You saw him *in* the Red Rotunda? In the same room where Gus died?'

Bee nodded.

'What's the article about?'

'Cranston being in hospital,' said Bee. 'Some kind of pancreatic cancer, I think. It was the first time he'd been seen for years. It sounds pretty bad. This quote from his doctor makes it sound like he was definitely going to die.'

'But he didn't.'

Bee looked at the top corner of the article. 'It's from early last year,' she said. 'So no, I guess he didn't.'

'Did Cranston look sick when you saw him? Like a man who's dying from cancer?'

Bee shook her head. 'He looked fine. Sad, but healthy.'

'And Gus was his *assistant*. Wow. So is this Cranston guy a suspect now?'

'I suppose so,' said Bee. 'But even if he is, it still doesn't answer the most important question.'

'And what's that?'

'What was this article doing pinned up in Adrian Featherstone's office?'

① ① ①

That evening, Bee took the clipping home with her and laid it on the desk in her bedroom.

Why had Gus changed his name? His work with Cranston wasn't on his CV, and he'd never mentioned it. It was almost as if he were trying to keep it a secret. As if he'd taken on a new identity.

Why? And what was Cranston doing in the Red Rotunda on the morning before Gus's death? William Cranston, a known recluse. Why the sudden urge to visit the museum? Had he been to see Gus? Did he say something to cause Gus to kill himself? Or did he murder Gus?

Bee shook her head. The front door slammed. Angela burst into the room and flopped on Bee's bed with a dramatic sigh.

'Hi, Mum.'

Angela sighed again through a smile and gazed at the ceiling. Bee rolled her eyes.

'So how was your date with Gavin?'

'Oh, Bee!' said Angela, her voice high and breathy. 'It was wonderful. He's just amazing. He's kind and intelligent and funny. We have so much in common it's uncanny. He even hates the new Star Wars films.'

'Mum, everyone hates the new Star Wars films.'

'Yes, darling. But he *really* hates them. He made a *website* about it. And we just talked and talked all through dinner and he was such a gentleman.'

'Where did you go?'

'Matsuya. We got that big boat full of sushi that you always said we should get, remember?'

Bee raised her eyebrows. 'Did he use chopsticks?'

Angela laughed. 'Of course he did. What a funny thing to ask.'

'It's just...how did he hold them? With his paws? I can't imagine it. I thought he'd be more likely to spear each piece of fish with one of those long claws and eat it that way.'

Bee's mum sat up. 'Very funny,' she said. 'You know I told you that Neal has a human form.'

'Who's Neal?'

'Gavin. His real name is Neal.'

Bee blinked. 'And he's not a badger.'

'No.'

'So he doesn't have a furry nose.'

'No.'

'Or long claws.'

'No.'

'Or whiskers.'

'I'm not sure if real badgers have whiskers. But in any case, no.'

'How disappointing.'

Angela stuck out her tongue. 'He wants to take me out again tonight, but I said I'd have to check with you first.'

'Well, I don't know, Angela,' said Bee. 'Have you done all your homework?'

'You were upset the other night,' said Angela. 'And I don't want to be gallivanting all over town with a nice man if you need maternal support and wise counsel.'

'Now that Gavin's not a Celestial Badger anymore, I don't see where I'm supposed to get any wise counsel from.'

'Seriously, Bee,' said her mother. 'Are you okay?'

'I'm fine. Go and call your badger and tell him he can take you out.'

Angela sprang up and kissed Bee on the top of her head. 'Thank you!' she said. 'Neal wants to take me to the Astor. They're showing *Labyrinth* tonight!'

'Have fun,' said Bee. 'Say hi to David Bowie's magic pants for me.'

'I will,' said Angela, and practically skipped out of the room.

Bee glanced at her mobile phone. There was another missed call from Maddy. And voicemail. Bee deleted it without listening and switched on her laptop.

7

'So I emailed my anatomy professor about Cranston,' said Toby on Wednesday morning. 'It turns out he's totally famous. My professor says he's been overlooked for a Nobel Prize like a hundred times. He did this thing with horseshoe crabs where he found they had crazy blue blood that clots when it encounters bacteria. Now they use it to test pharmaceuticals, and to check for bacterial diseases. They even use it on the International Space Station to test surfaces for bacteria and fungi. Are you even listening?'

'Hmm?' Bee looked up. 'Sure.'

'Aren't you interested in learning about Cranston? Or have we struck him from the list?'

'No, he's on the list,' said Bee. 'He's at the top of the list.'

'But you're not interested in what I learned about Cranston because…'

'Because I stayed up all night reading about him on the internet.'

Toby made a face of mock horror. 'You kids and your newfangled technology.'

Bee sighed.

'So what did *you* discover, Holmes?' asked Toby.

'Cranston is rich. Like, *really* rich. Family money. He owns a lot of property in the UK, but lives on this huge estate near Healesville. And you're right, he's totally famous in the science world for his work with the horseshoe crab. But he's also famous because he's a bit weird. He's a total recluse – he doesn't even have any living relatives. He never attends any charity functions or lectures or anything. He was awarded an AO but didn't turn up to collect it. I guess that's one of the reasons he lives in Australia instead of England – he doesn't have to meet fellow researchers and so on. Even the people who worked with him never met him. He employed people in labs all over the world and insisted they communicate via correspondence.'

'See? Nobody even talks to each other anymore.'

Bee gave him a look. 'So nobody heard anything of Cranston for years,' she continued. 'Except for that article we found in Adrian Featherstone's office about him being sick.'

'So he got better?'

'I guess so – he checked himself out of hospital after three days and went home. And nobody heard from him after that.'

'Except you saw him in the Red Rotunda.'

'The day that Gus died. And then I saw him again, sitting outside the museum, on the morning they found Gus's body.'

Toby took off his glasses. 'So Gus was working for Cranston,' he said. 'And Cranston was in the room where Gus was found dead, mere hours before the murder. Doesn't that kind of point towards...'

'Towards the possibility that Cranston knew about the murder before it happened.'

'Do you think he did it?'

Bee shrugged. 'I don't know. He must have been *involved* somehow, otherwise it's just too much of a coincidence. But what could his motive have been?'

'Maybe Cranston was mad that Gus came to work at the museum instead of remaining his assistant.'

'Maybe. But that still doesn't explain what Adrian Featherstone has to do with it.'

'Oh, and he *does* have something to do with it,' said Toby. 'I do not like that man *at all*. He's definitely involved.'

Bee looked absently at the clock on the wall. Who had changed the time back so it matched her watch?

'So is it time for the next step?' asked Toby.

'What next step?'

'In your detective methodology. Making a list of suspects.'

Bee blinked. 'I suppose so.'

'So who's on it?'

'Well, Cranston is currently at the top of the list. He has a connection with the victim and was present at the scene of the crime. Except I don't know what his motive could have been. He certainly can't have killed Gus for money. Revenge, maybe? For something Gus did?' She narrowed her eyes. 'Then there's Adrian Featherstone. He's hiding something. Why did he have that clipping on his pinboard? And I'm pretty sure I caught him going through Gus's desk the other day. And...'

'What?'

'I don't know. There's something else. I'm just not sure what it is. I think we have to find out what his connection to Cranston and Gus is. And see if he has an alibi.'

Toby grinned. Bee raised an eyebrow.

'Sorry,' said Toby. 'It's just in the last minute you've said *victim* and *scene of the crime* and *motive* and *alibi*. I feel like I'm in an episode of *Midsomer Murders*.'

'I feel like you're not taking this seriously.'

'Sorry,' Toby said again. 'Carry on. Any other suspects?'

Bee gave him a suspicious look. 'We should find out which security guard was on duty,' she said. 'Even if they're not a suspect, they might have seen or heard something. And I think we should also see what we can find out from Akiko Kobayashi.'

'You think she's a suspect?'

Bee shrugged. 'She might be able to shed some light on the whole Cranston–Gus–Featherstone thing.'

'So what first?'

'Let's have another look in the Red Rotunda.'

The Red Rotunda was as empty as ever.

'So this was Cranston's personal collection?' asked Toby, indicating the glass cases.

Bee nodded. 'He was fascinated with the inner workings of animals and how they compared to humans. He even preserved his own pet dog and cats for study.' She pointed at the mangy animals.

'Nice,' said Toby, squinting at the jar of mole paws.

Bee looked at the skeletons, jars and mounted specimens. What had they seen the other night, through their veils of glass and methylated spirits? Who else had been here in this room with Gus? If only they could tell her. If only it had been *her* eyes in Gus's pocket... Bee shook her head. She was going crazy.

'Hey,' said Toby. 'Here's the horseshoe crab.'

It was in a small glass case alongside an ugly black critter labelled DEATHSTALKER SCORPION *(Leiurus quinquestriatus)*, and several types of spider. Bee shuddered.

'They're actually very interesting creatures,' said Toby, still peering at the horseshoe crab. 'I did some reading last night after I talked to my professor. This is the closest living relative of the trilobite. And do you know how they mate?'

'No.'

'The male is smaller, and not as strong. So he climbs onto the back of the lady crab, holding on with his front claw, while she swims in to shore to lay her eggs. Sometimes he can hold on for months at a time.'

'Clingy.'

'It shows a certain dedication to the breeding process.'

'Or just laziness,' said Bee. 'He could have swum there himself.'

'Maybe,' said Toby, inching towards Bee. 'Maybe he just wanted to be close to her.'

Bee studied the horseshoe crab. It didn't look much like a crab at all, more like some kind of prehistoric armoured miniature stingray. She wondered how anyone could want to be close to anything that hard and spiky.

She could feel Toby's warmth next to her. He wasn't hard and spiky at all.

'It's weird, isn't it?' she said. 'How strange other species are. How different the boy crab is from the girl crab.'

'Like the difference between girl humans and boy humans?'

'Even more so, don't you think?' she said. 'I mean, we're mostly the same, right? On the inside. Apart from wombs and things, and some small structural variations. It's just culture that makes us seem so different.'

'Our hearts aren't the same,' said Toby. 'You can tell on an ECG. The intervals are a bit different. The funny thing is, if you put a man's heart into a woman, it'll start behaving like a woman's heart. But if you put a female heart into a male, it'll always beat like a woman's heart.'

He put one hand on his own chest, and pressed the other against Bee's, and closed his eyes in concentration. Bee wondered if he could feel her heart beating faster and faster as soon as he'd touched her. The somewhat sly grin on his face indicated that he could. Bee's cheeks grew hot. She wanted to lean forward and... but she knew she shouldn't. Toby didn't *really* like her. He was just a flirt. If he really liked her, he would have made it clear. He would have said something or done something after the incident on the tiger. And anyway, she was glad he didn't like her. Because she didn't like him.

'Come on,' she said, taking a step backwards so Toby's hand fell. 'Let's go and see Kobayashi.'

Museum Director Akiko Kobayashi was sitting at her desk studying a stapled sheaf of paper covered in tiny numbers. Bee and Toby waited in the doorway for her to notice them. She put a hand to her temple and closed her eyes with a sigh.

Toby knocked quietly on the doorframe to get her attention. Kobayashi jumped and opened her eyes.

'Sorry to interrupt,' said Toby. 'But we were wondering if we could have a word.'

Kobayashi looked flustered and a little annoyed, but she nodded and they sat on the other side of her desk. Bee noticed her slide a letter under another pile of papers.

Kobayashi peered at them through her narrow chrome-framed glasses. 'You again,' she said. 'Why do you always turn up at the most inconvenient of times?'

Toby seemed about to say something, then glanced at Bee and thought better of it.

Bee introduced herself and explained that she, too, had been working with Gus. Kobayashi's expression softened.

'Of course you were,' she said. 'And you must be very upset. I'm sorry if I was abrupt.' She gestured to the sheaf of paper. 'We have to submit the budget to the government next month, and it's rather like trying to add up every star in the sky using an abacus.'

'Is the museum having money trouble?' asked Toby, leaning forward and putting on his best concerned-and-supportive face.

'Well, that's one way to put it,' said Kobayashi. 'Natural history museums aren't as cool as they once were. Now it's all about science museums and immigration museums and sports museums. It's hard to attract private donors with so much glitzy competition.'

'Hey,' said Toby, gently. 'That must be really difficult. But if it helps, I think you're doing an amazing job. Natural history is so important. It's like...everything, right?'

Bee bit her lip to stop herself from rolling her eyes. Flirting seemed to be Toby's automatic reaction to any situation.

'But none of that need concern you,' said Kobayashi. 'What can I do for you both?'

'We wanted to ask about William Cranston,' said Bee.

'Did you see him last Thursday too?' said Kobayashi, brightening. 'How very exciting to have him here in our museum! It really is a great honour.'

'What's his relationship with the museum?' asked Bee.

Kobayashi smiled. 'He has been one of our most generous benefactors,' she said. 'He's donated funds to this museum for the past fifty years, as well as his own collection, which you may have seen in the Red Rotunda.'

They nodded.

'And of course he's an amazing scientist, a living legend in the field of natural history. Such an inspiration. We thought we might have lost him last year...'

A funny expression passed across Kobayashi's face. Bee thought it might be...disappointment? Then Kobayashi smiled again. 'But thankfully he seems to be totally recovered. Such a blessing.' She looked at Bee and Toby. 'Why do you want to know about him?'

'We think that he might be connected—' Toby started, but Bee kicked him in the ankle.

'Toby's a fan,' she said, rolling her eyes and picking up a glass paperweight from Kobayashi's desk. 'He's studying to be a zoologist, and he never stops going on about Cranston. It's all "William Cranston this" and "William Cranston that". I'm sure he's got a poster on his wall that he kisses every night before going to sleep. Anyway, we were just wondering if he's likely to come back to the museum, so Toby can get his autograph.'

Bee toyed with the paperweight as Toby shot her a puzzled scowl. Kobayashi laughed. 'Well, he's *very* reclusive, as I'm sure you know. This was the first time I'd ever heard of him actually visiting the museum in person. So I'm not sure if we'll see him again. I can't even imagine what brought him here. Just seeing what we're up to, I suppose. I'm disappointed I was in a meeting all day and didn't get to speak to him. I didn't even learn he was here until after he'd left.'

Bee nodded and then dropped the paperweight. 'Sorry!' she said and peered down at the carpet. The paperweight rolled under Kobayashi's chair. Looking slightly peeved, Kobayashi leaned down to pick it up. Bee quickly slid the letter out from under the pile and stuck it up her top. Toby raised his eyebrows.

Bee stood. 'Well, thanks for talking to us. I'm sure you're very busy.'

'One more question,' Toby said to Kobayashi. 'Can you tell me how long Adrian Featherstone's been the head of Conservation?'

'Just over a year, I think,' said Kobayashi. 'Why do you ask?'

Toby shook his head. 'I just thought I'd seen him somewhere before,' he said. 'But it must have been someone else.'

Once they'd left the office, he rounded on Bee.

'You stole a document from her office,' he said, indignant. 'That's so my job!'

'I think we have to add her to the suspect list,' said Bee.

'What?' said Toby. 'Why?'

'I don't want to talk here,' said Bee, eyeing a secretary who was pretending to be working on a spreadsheet, but was actually updating her Facebook status.

They found a quiet corner of the museum café, and ordered drinks. Bee extracted the letter and read it a few times.

By the time the waitress brought Toby his milkshake and Bee her coffee, Toby was nearly purple with impatience.

'Tell me what's going on,' he said. 'Why is Kobayashi a suspect? She didn't even mention Gus. What's in that letter?'

'It's from a law firm,' said Bee. 'It's a response to a request for funding. The letter says that their client isn't going to give them any money at this time.'

'So?'

'Listen to this. "Rest assured that on the unhappy occasion of Doctor Cranston's demise, once his dependants

94

have been provided for, a generous sum will be bequeathed to the museum."'

'It's from Cranston's lawyer?'

Bee nodded. 'I bet Cranston's fortune would easily solve the museum's money trouble.'

'Then why kill Gus?' asked Toby. 'Surely she'd kill Cranston.'

Bee stirred another spoon of sugar into her coffee. 'Well, Gus and Cranston look pretty close in that photo, don't they? And the letter said *once his dependants have been provided for.* Cranston doesn't have any family.'

Toby nodded and slurped up the rest of his milkshake. 'So Gus was in his will too. And with Gus out of the picture, the museum gets *more* money when Cranston dies.'

'And Cranston's already sick,' said Bee. 'Did you see her face when she was talking about that? It looked like she *wanted* him to die. That newspaper article said his condition was terminal, so surely it's just a matter of time. And now Gus is out of the way...'

'So the museum gets the whole package.' He looked around. 'This café could certainly use a facelift.'

'It would mean that Kobayashi knew that Gus was really Gregory Uriel Swindon.'

'Do you think that's possible?'

95

Bee shrugged. 'It would explain how he got the job with such a sketchy CV and a fabricated former employer.'

'She doesn't look like a killer.'

'No,' said Bee. 'And statistically it's pretty unlikely. Eighty-eight per cent of murders are committed by men.'

Toby shook his head. 'We're pigs,' he said. 'It's a mathematical fact.'

Bee flashed him a grin, then became serious again. 'I don't know, though,' she said. 'Kobayashi is clearly very passionate about the museum. And if its money trouble is as severe as she made it sound...who knows what steps she'd take to secure its future? We certainly shouldn't discount her just because she's a woman.'

'So how come you didn't ask her for an alibi?'

Bee screwed up her nose. 'I don't think you can just *ask*,' she said. 'Not in real life. You don't casually saunter into someone's office and say *Where were you on the night of January 13?* People get offended. And if she really did murder Gus, we hardly want her to know we suspect her.'

'So how do we find out?'

'I don't know. I guess we have to be sneaky.'

Toby tied the straw from his milkshake into a knot. 'What about Featherstone?' he asked. 'Where does he come into it?'

'I don't know.' Bee sighed. 'We're missing something. Something big.'

ⓘ ⓘ ⓘ

There was a list on the fridge when Bee got home.

THINGS TO NOTE

1. As you may be aware, I have a gentleman friend.
2. His name is Neal.
3. He is not a badger, but in fact a Real Live Person.
4. I like him.
5. A lot.
6. I have invited him over for dinner tonight.
7. As I would like him to meet my lovely daughter.
8. (That's you.)
9. Please join us at seven o'clock for food.
10. If you're comfortable with it, that is. If not, I totally understand.
11. But I'd really like you to.
12. With love,
13. Your mother.
14. Xxxxx
15. PS Don't worry, I won't cook.

Bee scowled at the note. Stupid Celestial Badger. Why did her mum have to get a new boyfriend anyway? Bee hadn't liked any of the others, so she found it difficult to see how this one would be any different. But Angela had asked nicely and it wasn't as if there was anywhere else Bee could go. The tiny voice in a dark corner of her head suggested calling Toby to see what his plans for the evening entailed, but she hushed it.

Bee checked her email, but logged out when she saw there was a message from Maddy. Instead, she picked up a James Ellroy novel and automatically turned its pages without taking anything in, until she heard the front door open, and voices in the hallway. Her mother's laugh was high and girlish, and it made Bee squirm inside. She took a few deep breaths and opened her door.

A man was standing at the kitchen bench with his back to Bee. He was quite short and skinny. Angela was clearing plates and bowls out of the dishwasher. She was wearing something low-cut and purple, with her hair all twisted back and great clusters of silver dangling from her ears.

'Bee!' she said, her voice breathless. 'This is Neal.'

The Celestial Badger turned, a bottle of wine in one hand. He was a small, timid-looking Asian man with silver-rimmed glasses and a pudding-bowl haircut. He ducked his head in greeting and said 'Hi' in a quiet, shaky voice.

'It's nice to meet you,' Bee said, taking in his neat but clearly inexpensive polyester suit, digital watch and slightly trembling hands. He had no pale band on his ring finger, so he wasn't married and hadn't been recently. Well, that was an improvement on the last guy. The Badger looked to be in his late twenties, which was a good ten years younger than Angela. Interesting.

Bee helped spread containers of takeaway on the table, then poured herself a glass of water and sat at the table.

'The naan is really good,' Angela told Neal. 'I hope you like Indian food.'

Neal smiled nervously. 'I do,' he said. 'As long as it's not too hot.'

Bee suppressed a smile. Angela liked her food as spicy as possible. During a chilli face-off at a science-fiction convention, she'd made a quite famous vindaloo chef cry.

'I ordered mild,' said Angela with a soppy smile.

Bee bit savagely into a pappadum, sending fragments of deep-fried chickpea flour all over the table. Angela looked reproachfully at her, then turned to Neal and began a long conversation about Dungeons and Dragons that involved a complicated analysis of something called psionics and how it related to divine and arcane magic, with lots of gooey eyes and hand-touching in between.

Bee tuned out and made a mental list of questions.

1. Why had Cranston suddenly started visiting the museum?
2. Why was he such a recluse?
3. What had his relationship with Gus been like?
4. Why did Gus have a handful of glass eyes in his pocket?
5. Why had Gus been acting so strangely the day he died?
6. What the hell was Adrian Featherstone's deal?
7. Why did he act like such a creep?
8. What was *his* relationship with Gus?
9. Had he known Gus before Gus came to the museum?
10. Did he know Cranston?

It all kept coming back to Cranston. William Cranston, the reclusive scientific genius, who kept getting overlooked for a Nobel Prize. William Cranston, employer of Gus. Benefactor of the museum. Bee had to speak to him. The puzzle had about a hundred missing pieces, but Bee reckoned at least seventy of them were to do with Cranston. Could he have killed Gus? It seemed unlikely.

Cranston was an old man – and one who had recently been very ill. Surely he couldn't be strong enough to have overpowered Gus in a struggle. But then, Gus had been a pretty frail guy himself.

Bee suddenly became aware that Angela and the Celestial Badger were staring at her.

'Sorry,' she said. 'What?'

A brief frown flickered over Angela's face. 'Neal asked you a question, Bee.'

'I'm sorry, Gav— sorry, Neal,' said Bee, flashing a smile that she hoped was warm. 'My mind had wandered. What did you say?'

The Celestial Badger brushed his pudding-bowl fringe back from his brow, which was beaded with sweat. Either the Badger was very nervous, or even the mild curry was a challenge for him. Or both. 'I was just asking about your summer job. Angela says you're working in a museum.'

Bee nodded. 'The Natural History Museum. I'm working in the taxidermy lab helping with a new exhibition on native fauna.'

'Taxidermy?' said the Badger, screwing up his nose. 'Like stuffing animals?'

'We call it mounting,' said Bee. 'And also some freeze-drying. There are other departments that do bones and fabricated creatures.'

'Isn't it disgusting?'

Bee shrugged. 'Not really,' she said. 'We have to be very careful about hygiene. It's not like we're dealing with rotting corpses or anything. Every animal is frozen until we need to use it. Then once the inside bits are discarded we're just working with a dry skin.'

The Badger shuddered. 'You must be very brave.'

'I'm just not afraid of dead things,' said Bee. 'And I like the way we can sort of bring them back to life. I mean, they don't run around and smell and eat anymore, but people still get to enjoy them.'

'Fair enough.' The Badger still looked dubious.

'So what do you do, Neal?' said Bee, sure it would be something incredibly dull.

'I'm an accountant,' the Badger replied, giving Bee a little thrill of satisfaction.

'Now *there* is something you need to be brave to do,' said Bee. 'Surrounded by nothing but numbers all day. I can't think of anything worse.'

'More wine?' interrupted Angela, shooting a warning glance at Bee. She refilled Neal's glass and her own. Bee sipped pointedly from her glass of water, and then put down her fork.

'It's been lovely meeting you,' she said to Neal with a smile. 'But I've got an early start tomorrow and I need to get some reading done. I'll leave you guys alone.'

Neal fumbled with his wine glass and napkin as he awkwardly stood up. The wine spilled, drowning his curry. He blushed pink to the tip of his nose and dropped his napkin into the soggy mess on his plate, then wiped his hand on his trousers before holding it out for Bee to shake.

'N-nice to meet you too,' he said, looking as though he might burst into tears.

'Night, Mum,' said Bee to her mother, who had rushed into the kitchen for paper towel.

Back in her room, Bee tried once again to read her novel, and failed. She prowled around for a while, putting away clean clothes, and finally turned her computer back on. She swallowed and double-clicked on Maddy's email.

Hey,

I hope you had a great Christmas and Santa brought you everything you wanted.

So. Remember the last day of school? When we all went to that party at Sam Mitchell's house? And you left early because you had to work the next day? Well, I stayed. And I probably drank a bit too much, which was dumb. But I got talking to Fletch, and stuff happened. By which I mean we ended up kissing on the couch.

I didn't mean for it to happen, and I'm so, so sorry. I know that's no excuse, and there's REALLY no excuse for what happened next.

I called Fletch and asked him to have a coffee with me, so we could figure out what to tell you. Except it didn't really work out that way, because it happened again. And again. It's been happening all summer.

I know I'm a first-grade lowlife scumbag harridan. But here's the thing: I like Fletch. I really like him, and he really likes me. And you never said it out loud, but I know you and he were only ever lukewarm. I know you found him a bit boring, and I know he never really 'got' you.

I'm so sorry for being such a weasel about this. But if there's anything I can do at all that will help you forgive me, then just name it. Anything! Except give him up. I'm afraid that's the one thing I just can't do.

Yours in weaselly, sucky, terrible-friendish love,

Maddy xxxxxxx

Bee shut her laptop and gazed at the wall for a moment, wondering if she was going to cry. After a few minutes it became clear that she wasn't, so she pulled on her pyjamas and climbed into bed. She wasn't sure she felt anything – not anger or hurt or betrayal. Perhaps she was just in shock, or perhaps Maddy was right and she'd never cared much for Fletch after all. She wondered absently what Toby was doing, and how she might get to Cranston. She was just formulating a plan when sleep came. Cranston could wait until morning.

9

BEE TRIED THE OBVIOUS FIRST, and looked up Cranston in the phone directory. No joy. Then she tried googling 'Cranston' and 'Healesville', but all she got were news articles containing vague references to Cranston's fortune and his large country estate. It was time to be more sneaky.

She dialled the number for the Healesville local council. A man answered.

'Hi,' said Bee. 'My name's Samantha Teal. I'm a professional exterminator and I've been given a job at the residence of a man called William Cranston. Apparently it's quite a big job, but I've run into a problem. The address I've been given isn't correct, and I was wondering if you could help me.'

There was a pause on the other end of the phone. 'You don't have a contact phone number you can try?'

Bee thought quickly. 'Nobody's answering.'

Another pause. 'Could you tell me the number?'

'Um,' said Bee. '5293 4444.'

'Guess again,' said the man. 'Tell your English friend I'm not going to be fooled just because he gets a girl to call. We don't give out private addresses *or* phone numbers.'

The line went dead. English friend? Could he have meant Featherstone?

Bee tried Facebook, but she knew it was a lost cause. As if Cranston would be on Facebook. She frowned, pulled on her dressing-gown and headed out of her room in search of breakfast. How did you find someone who didn't want to be found? *Why* didn't he want to be found, anyway? And who else was looking for him?

Bee barely noticed the Celestial Badger sitting at the table, his shirt untucked and wrinkled, and his hair all tousled. He was drinking coffee from a mug and reading the newspaper, and he sat bolt upright and blushed when Bee emerged.

'Um,' he said, his voice barely above a whisper. 'Good morning.'

'Hey,' said Bee distractedly, as she poured herself a glass of pineapple juice.

'Y-your mother's in the shower.'

'Uh-huh.' Bee sipped her juice. Was there someone else she could call? Did Cranston have any employees

107

who she might track down? He must have a cleaner, or a handyman. She could call every cleaner and handyman in the Healesville area.

The Celestial Badger screwed up his courage. 'I know this must be difficult for you,' he said, everything tumbling out in a rush. 'But I want you to know that I really like your mother. She's a very special lady and I know she's your mum and that must be weird, so I hope that you and I can be friends and if you don't want that then it's fine, but I hope at least we can get along, otherwise it's going to make things very difficult.'

Bee blinked at Neal. What was he talking about?

'Well?' he said, a little belligerently.

'What would you do if you had to find someone?' she asked. 'If all you knew was their name, but you had to find them.'

The Badger looked taken aback, but he seemed to conclude that if Bee was asking him questions like this, she was probably okay with him sleeping over.

'Have you tried the electoral roll?' he asked.

'No,' said Bee. 'How can I see it? Is it available to the public?'

The Celestial Badger nodded eagerly. 'It sure is,' he said. 'You just go into your local electoral office and they have a kiosk where you can look up anyone's name. If they're on the roll, their address will be there.'

'Really?' said Bee. 'Everyone's address? Just available to anyone?'

'Unless someone's specifically asked not to be listed,' said Neal. 'Like, Kylie Minogue would probably have her address suppressed, because she runs a risk of being stalked.'

'Huh,' said Bee. 'Thanks!'

She disappeared back into her room to get changed, leaving the Celestial Badger looking confused but pleased.

As Bee headed out the front door, her mother stopped her. 'Sweetheart,' she said, 'are you okay? With Neal sleeping over? I meant to talk to you first, but it sort of…happened somewhat unexpectedly. I'm really sorry I didn't discuss it with you.'

Bee grinned. 'It's fine, Mum,' she said. 'He was very helpful.' She breezed past and out into the street.

She bought herself a coffee and a croissant from a little French bakery, and then waited for the Electoral Office to open, which it did at 10:02 AM.

A friendly looking young man with curly dark hair was behind a counter tapping at a computer. He smiled at Bee and she nodded back at him, but turned to the line of computer kiosks on her left. She clicked SEARCH on one monitor, then typed CRANSTON, WILLIAM into the box and selected VIC from the pull-down menu.

The computer paused for a moment, and Bee held her breath. Then a list flickered over the screen. There were only four Cranstons in Victoria, and only one William. Bee's heart sank. Where the other three Cranstons had a full address, postcode and electorate, the entry for William Cranston had only two words: ADDRESS SUPPRESSED.

Bee scowled at the computer, and then glanced over to the friendly man. She carefully assembled her most vulnerable facial expression, and approached him with a timid smile.

'Um, hi,' she said, looking demurely down at her hands.

'Hey,' said the young man. 'Can I help you with something?'

Bee nodded shyly. 'I'm trying to get some details for someone,' she said, 'but when I look him up it says the address is suppressed.'

'That means he's a silent elector,' said the man. 'He's requested that his address not be made public.'

'You can do that?'

The man shrugged. 'Yes, if you can demonstrate that making your address public would constitute a threat to you.'

Bee let her lower lip tremble. 'So there's no way of finding his address?'

'Sorry.'

Bee had taught herself to cry when she was seven. It had taken her several months of staring into the bathroom mirror and thinking about how her goldfish had died and her mother had flushed it down the toilet without letting Bee say goodbye first. But after intensive practice, Bee could bring on the tears at will, without even having to think about little Herman Melville and his swishy orange tail.

'Um,' she said, her voice going high and squeaky as her eyes filled with tears. 'I'm sorry. It's just... I found out a few days ago that my dad isn't my real dad.' Bee paused for some dramatic gulpy breathing. 'And my mum finally told me who my real dad is, but she's not in contact with him anymore and all I have is a name and... I just want to meet him.'

'I'm really sorry,' said the young man. 'But I couldn't give it to you even if I was willing to break the law. Only the District Returning Officer has access to the silent elector details.'

'Th-the District Returning Officer? Is he here?'

A flicker of a frown passed over the young man's face. 'Do you know what electorate this man lives in?'

'I-I think he lives in Healesville.'

'That's McEwen,' said the man. 'Only the McEwen DRO would have access to those records. And don't get too excited,' he said, looking at Bee with sharp eyes. 'She won't be able to help you. It's a federal offence to give that information away. We can't even give it to the courts or the police.'

Bee pulled a tissue out of her handbag and sniffed. 'I just really need to find him.' She leaned towards the man and lowered her voice. 'I-I'm dying,' she whispered. 'I need a kidney transplant and he's the only chance I have at finding a match.'

The young man shook his head. 'Nice try, Veronica Mars,' he said. 'But I'm not an idiot. Have a great day.'

Bee spent the ten-minute walk to the museum composing a rant about how frustrated she was with the search for Cranston. She planned to deliver it to Toby, who would surely respond with *a*) sympathy or *b*) a breakthrough. Or preferably he would say something that would trigger *Bee* to have the breakthrough. That would be extra satisfactory.

But Toby wasn't in the taxidermy lab. The lights were off and nothing had moved since the night before. Bee checked the clock on the wall. Toby was nearly two hours late for work, which was pretty much inexcusable. Bee was also late, but now Toby didn't need to know that. Bee's irritation deepened. She couldn't find Cranston *and* she couldn't rant to Toby about it. And he was late. Again. Did he have no respect for his employer? That was probably why he needed to make up extra credit for uni. Extreme tardiness.

Bee pulled a seagull out of a plastic tub labelled SEA BIRDS and examined it critically. Its feathers had become all crumpled and untidy and a brown stain had appeared on one wing. Bee sighed.

When Toby finally came through the lab door, Bee was blowdrying the now-spotless seagull's feathers into place with a hairdryer.

'Hey,' said Toby, dropping his bag under his desk and plonking himself down on the chair. Bee ignored him and continued to blast the seagull.

'Thinking of opening a salon?' said Toby, raising his voice to be heard over the hairdryer. 'You could call it "Curly Bird Gets the Perm".'

Bee shot him a withering look.

'Yikes,' said Toby, and turned on his computer.

Bee switched off the hairdryer and put the much-neatened seagull on her desk

'And *where* have you been?' she snapped.

Toby looked taken aback. 'At uni,' he said. 'I had a meeting.'

'Uni?' asked Bee. 'Uni doesn't start until February. What was this *meeting* about?'

'If you recall,' said Toby, 'I'm here to make up extra credit because I failed an exam last year. I had a meeting with my anatomy professor to discuss my work here, and explain that he won't get a progress report from Gus when I'm done. Because Gus is dead.'

Bee stared at the seagull, who fixed her with a beady glass eye. She swallowed. 'Sorry,' she said, smoothing a wing feather. 'I'm just in a bad mood. I've been trying to track down Cranston all morning, and I can't seem to make any headway. It's like he doesn't want to be found.'

'Well, he doesn't,' said Toby. 'That's the definition of a recluse.'

'But *why?*' said Bee. 'Why is he a recluse?'

Toby shrugged. 'Some people just don't like people.'

'I suppose not.'

'So what now?'

Bee sighed. 'I don't know. I just need to find Cranston. I have a feeling that he's the key to all of this.'

'So what's the problem?'

'I can't *find* him!' Bee explained about the electoral roll and the phone book. 'I'm *that* close to catching a train to Healesville and wandering dirt roads, knocking on all the doors of the really big houses.'

'I reckon there are a few things we can try before it gets to that.'

'Good luck,' said Bee. 'I've tried every trick in my detective book.'

Toby grinned. 'Well, maybe it's time for the Worthy Beginner to step up to the plate.'

Bee gave him a flat look.

'Give me the number of the local council.'

'I already tried them,' said Bee. 'It didn't work.'

'Just give me the number.'

Bee read it out to him, and Toby picked up the phone and dialled. 'Good morning,' he said in a surprisingly convincing American accent. 'Can you please put me through to accounts receivable?' He paused and winked at Bee. 'Hello? Hey, yeah. I work for William Cranston, and I haven't received our annual rates bill yet. Can I please check the address you have for us is correct?' He mimed writing at Bee and she pushed a pen and paper towards him. 'Uh-huh,' he said, looking delighted. Then his face fell. 'Awesome. Yes, that's correct. Thanks.'

He hung up the phone. Bee raised her eyebrows. 'What was with the American accent?'

'Isn't that part of detecting? I'm hoping tomorrow you'll have to wear a blue wig and run around in a black vinyl catsuit.'

'You watch too much television.'

'DVD. Television is for amateurs.'

'Whatever. Did they tell you anything?'

He gave her the piece of paper and Bee's heart sank. 'It's a post office box,' she said. 'That doesn't help at all.'

'We could send him a letter,' suggested Toby half-heartedly.

'I suppose. But I don't really think that'd help.'

'What would Nancy Drew do? Use her feminine wiles?'

Bee shrugged. 'Probably. But I've got no one to wile.'

'Maybe you should practise on me.'

Bee chose not to respond.

Toby tapped a pen against his cheek. 'You want to hear about snails?'

'I'm sorry?'

'Snails,' said Toby. 'Did you know that most snails are hermaphrodites? So there's no lady snails and man snails, and they've all got double the bits.'

Bee tried to ignore him in the hope that he'd shut up eventually.

'So when two snails meet, they engage in this incredibly complicated and beautiful courtship dance. They circle around each other for ages, sometimes up to six or seven hours. And they touch each other's mouths and tentacles.'

'Ew.'

'It's really quite beautiful. Then when the foreplay is getting all exciting, one of the snails shoots a love dart at the other snail.'

'Is that some kind of disgusting euphemism?' asked Bee, who had become interested despite her very best efforts.

Toby shook his head. 'No, they literally shoot a dart. Like a tiny harpoon. Then the other snail shoots a dart into the first snail about half an hour later.' He looked meaningfully at Bee. 'Because when you're sharing a special moment, there's no need to rush things. Anyway, the love darts indicate that the snails are ready to move past foreplay. Then they both extend their penises, which, by the way, are pretty enormous, relatively speaking, and they kind of twirl them around each other and exchange sperm.'

'Charming.'

'It's quite extraordinary,' Toby continued. 'And possibly explains the snail's place in folklore.'

'What – being slow to get things going?'

Toby gave Bee a disappointed look. 'I feel that you're failing to fully appreciate the beauty of nature here.

Snails have fascinated people for centuries. Girls used to persuade boys they fancied to carry snail shells around in order to win their love. And gypsies thought that a snail shell was a charm against witchcraft, because snails were lucky enough to be able to give and take pleasure at the same time.'

Bee shook her head. 'Snails ate all our basil last summer. They are slimy and gross and not at all sexy.'

'Patricia Highsmith might disagree with you,' said Toby. 'Or at least she would if she were still alive.'

'Patricia Highsmith?' said Bee. 'The novelist? Who wrote *Strangers on a Train?*'

Toby chuckled. 'I thought you might know her,' he said. 'She being such an excellent author of psychological thrillers. Right up your alley.'

'What does Patricia Highsmith have to do with snails?'

'Oh, she loved them,' said Toby. 'She used to carry a handful around with her in her handbag whenever she travelled. They were her tiny friends who made her feel less alone. When she travelled overseas she used to tuck them under her breasts to get them past security.'

Bee's mouth fell open. 'Are you... Is this supposed to be... Are you trying to *turn me on* right now?'

'Is it working?'

118

'I wish there were more letters in the alphabet to express the emphaticness of my *no*.'

Toby grinned at her. 'What about if I told you that the Spanish word for "snail" is the same as their word for "vagina"?'

Bᴇᴇ ᴘᴜᴢᴢʟᴇᴅ ᴏᴠᴇʀ ꜰɪɴᴅɪɴɢ Cʀᴀɴsᴛᴏɴ as she carefully attached glass eyes to a stuffed platypus.

Toby was also unusually quiet, working on inserting structural wire and cottonwool into a koala. After an hour, Bee started to feel uncomfortable. Being alone in a room with Toby was...intense. She could feel his presence, hear his breathing. She flinched every time he bent down to get more cottonwool, sure that he was going to roll his chair over to her desk and say something flirty about the breeding habits of the platypus. But nothing. After two hours, Bee thought she might go crazy unless the silence was broken.

'So,' she said. 'Platypuses. Is it true they have a poisonous spike?'

Toby looked up. 'Venomous,' he corrected. 'The males have a venomous spike in their hind legs. They're one of only a handful of venomous mammals. Most of the others are shrews, and then there's some debate about whether the slow loris should be classed as venomous or poisonous. And some researchers say the skunk is poisonous, but most think it's just gross.'

He turned back to his koala. Bee ground her teeth with impatience.

'Platypi do have ten sex chromosomes, though,' said Toby suddenly, and Bee breathed a sigh of relief.

'Oh?'

'We only have two, like almost all other mammals. So mine are XY and yours are XX. A male platypus has XYXYXYXYXY.'

'What does that mean?'

Toby shrugged. 'It's complicated.'

Bee scowled at Toby. 'Are you okay?' she said. 'You're being very quiet today.'

'I'm fine,' he said. 'Just a bit tired.'

Bee stared down at the platypus. He'd probably been out at some undergrad party all night. With booze and girls. University girls, who were all experienced and confident and eager to explore the fringy boundaries of their sexuality. Bee hated every single one of them.

'Damn,' said Toby, and threw his pair of pliers onto his desk. 'Damn you, stupid *Phascolarctos cinereus*! You damned thickset arboreal marsupial herbivore! I curse you and all of your extinct *Phascolarctida* relatives. May every gumleaf you pick shrivel in your paw.'

Bee felt something inside her wobble. Toby *was* a little bit adorable. She went over to his desk. A piece of wire used for shaping the koala's jaw had unravelled, ripping its cheek open from eye to mouth.

'Do you think I can sew it closed?' Toby asked.

'Not unless you want to frighten children with a koala that looks like the Joker,' said Bee. 'You'll have to start over with a new skin.'

'There's another koala skin?'

Bee shook her head.

'So how do I start over?'

'Follow me.'

Bee took Toby down a corridor to a large metal door. She unlocked it with one of Gus's keys, and pushed it open. There was a sucking noise and a gust of cold air.

'This is the freezer,' she explained. 'It's where we keep all the animals.'

Toby looked around, fascinated, as they walked between two shelves stacked with frozen bundles of fur. A box was marked MICE, another TOADS AND FROGS. Every animal had a small yellow tag hanging off it, marking its species, weight and the date it was brought in, along with its collection number.

As they rounded the corner of one shelved aisle, Toby yelped in surprise.

'There's a *lion*,' he said, pointing.

Bee nodded and reached out a hand to touch the icy golden fur. 'He came in the same week I started here,' she said. 'He's from the zoo. When a lion gets really old, the younger lions tear him apart, which isn't so nice for all the visiting kiddies to see. So they euthanased this one and sent him here.'

Bee remembered the way Gus had stroked the fur of the dead lion as he told Bee about the zoo and the other lions. There had been something incredibly respectful in his tone. Bee had gently touched the lion's mane too, and seen how thick and wild it must have once been. She swallowed as she realised she missed Gus. She missed him sitting at his desk, working away in silence.

'What will happen to him?' asked Toby. 'Will he go on display?'

Bee shrugged. 'Maybe, if there's an exhibition that needs a lion. Otherwise he'll just stay down here until we need him. There are nearly seven million items in storage at this museum, and less than ten thousand on display at any time.'

She bent over at one of the bottom shelves.

'Male or female?' she asked.

'Male,' said Toby.

Bee hauled out a furry grey corpse and handed it to Toby. He nearly dropped it, not expecting it to be so heavy.

'Um,' he said. 'Not that I am in any way weirded out by all this, but how exactly am I supposed to detach the inside of this koala from the outside?'

'Don't you know?' Bee said. 'I thought you were studying medicine?'

Toby blinked. 'Yes. Well. Oddly enough there doesn't seem to be much call for the removal of a patient's skin these days.'

'You haven't done dissection?'

'No. It's complicated. Let's say it's one of the reasons why I'm here.'

Bee rolled her eyes. 'There's a manual you can use,' she said. 'We do it in the wet area of the lab, near the sink. You wait for a couple of hours so the very outside thaws, but not the inside because then things get too messy. You cut open its belly, not too deep because you don't want it to bleed much. Then you loosen the skin with a blunt knife, and disarticulate the legs.'

'*Disarticulate the legs?*'

'Is there a problem?'

'No,' said Toby, looking a little grey. 'What happens after the legs are no longer articulated?'

'Well, a koala doesn't have much of a tail, so you don't have to worry about that. So once you've done the back legs, you hang him up on the pulley and pull off the rest of his skin.'

'Hang him...on the *pulley*?'

'Are you seriously going to repeat every word I say?'

'No.'

Bee scowled at him. 'Well, we might just start you on that. I'll help you when you get to the head. It's pretty complicated.'

'Did Gus teach you all this?'

'Yep. He was a good teacher.'

'And you seem like a fast learner.'

Bee shrugged. 'I like to learn.'

Toby regarded his koala. 'So then what? Once I've... skinned him?'

'We don't need the skeleton, so we'll chuck that away,' said Bee. 'Then you just have to preserve the skin so it stops decaying.'

Toby brightened. 'Scary chemical time?'

'Sorry,' said Bee. 'Just salt.'

'Salt?'

'Salt.'

'Is it at least some kind of special salt? With a fancy name?'

'Generic salt from the supermarket,' said Bee. 'We don't use any of the nasty stuff…' She trailed off.

'Are you okay?'

'We don't use toxic chemicals for preservation! We don't even *have* any.'

Bee turned and ran back to the taxidermy lab. Toby hefted his koala and came after her. She was already sitting at her desk and staring at a Wikipedia page on her computer.

'I'm an idiot,' she said. 'A total idiot.'

'What? Why?'

She turned to Toby. 'The vial Gus was holding in his hand. The label said it was corrosive sublimate. That's an old name for mercuric chloride, which is a preservative chemical. That's why nobody questioned Gus's suicide, because they all figured he'd have total access to all sorts of deadly chemicals. Except he didn't. Museums haven't used mercuric chloride for at least a hundred years. Nobody uses it anymore, because it's so dangerous.'

Toby frowned. 'Then how did he get it?'

'Maybe someone else administered it. But where would anyone get it from?'

'I think I might know,' said Toby. 'Come with me.'

126

Bee frowned. 'You can't just leave the koala on your desk. It'll go stinky.'

'He'll be okay for ten minutes,' said Toby. 'Just come *on*.'

He led Bee out of the Catacombs, up the stairs into the museum and over to a case in a dingy corner near the Red Rotunda.

'Oh,' said Bee. '*Oh*.'

The case was an often-overlooked memorial to the museum's history. It contained a few photos of the museum in the late 1800s, including one of Queen Victoria standing beside an Australian coat of arms made from a taxidermied kangaroo and emu; a mangy, moth-eaten platypus; and a line of quaint little bottles containing deadly chemicals. Next to the square card labelled Corrosive Sublimate or Mercuric Chloride, there was no bottle.

Bee looked up at Toby. 'Well, that answers where it came from,' she said. 'But who took it?'

'It *could* have been Gus,' said Toby. 'He'd have access to these cabinets.'

'Anyone who works here could gain access,' said Bee. 'It's not that hard to get the key to a cabinet from Security.'

'So does that rule out Cranston?' asked Toby. 'He wouldn't have been able to get in there without someone noticing and causing a fuss.'

'Maybe.' Bee studied the case, her head on one side. 'But I don't want to cross him off the list just yet.'

'So now what?'

'I think it's time we talked to Security.'

Roy Cantwell was the head of Security. He seemed initially suspicious when Bee asked him who had been on duty the night of Gus's death, but she flirted a little and became distraught whenever she mentioned Gus, and in the end Roy was so worried she was going to burst into tears that he told her. Faro Costa had been the security guard that night, and he would be on duty again that afternoon.

Bee and Toby found Faro, twenty minutes before his shift started, smoking a cigarette outside the museum.

Faro Costa was a well-built, good-looking man in his late fifties. He had broad shoulders and dark hair cropped close to his head. A snake tattoo coiled around his forearm, its forked tongue licking his palm. Around his neck was a bronze pendant that looked like a tree all twisted in on itself.

Bee knew Faro reasonably well – he'd let her into the building one morning when she had forgotten her smartcard, and he'd told her in his clipped European accent all about his theory of where the taxidermied animals' souls went. He was...eccentric, but Bee liked him and had always found time to say hello whenever she saw him. There was something incredibly gentle about him, despite the snake tattoo, and Bee was tempted to drop him from the suspect list.

She explained that she wanted to know about what had happened the night of Gus's death.

'Why?' asked Faro. 'It is dangerous to dwell in the past. The past is full of shadows. They can snatch you up and steal your soul.'

Toby glanced sideways at Bee.

'Stay in the light,' said Faro. 'In the land of the living. Gus has gone from this land. He is in a better place.'

'I very much doubt that,' muttered Toby.

'But I think it would help *me*,' said Bee. 'With closure. I have so many questions.'

Faro inhaled deeply on his cigarette. 'Some questions cannot be answered by men. You should come to my church. I find the answers to all my questions there.'

Toby gave an audible snort and Bee glared at him. 'Thanks,' she said. 'But I really need to know.'

Faro shook his head sadly. 'The land of shadows is thick about you,' he said. 'Come back into the light.'

'Just tell him,' said Toby. 'Tell him the truth.'

Bee hesitated. She was sure Faro Costa couldn't be the murderer...but could she really tell him all her suspicions? Poirot certainly wouldn't, but Poirot was extremely irksome, so perhaps she *should* just tell Faro. Especially if he *had* seen something that might help them.

'Fine,' said Bee, and turned back to Faro. 'We think Gus might have been murdered.' She told him about Cranston and Gus's relationship with him, and about the pocketful of eyes, the smartcard, the missing mercuric chloride and the noise they'd heard in the lab at twenty to one on the night of the murder. Faro listened carefully.

'The police?' he asked finally. 'Have you told them?'

'I tried,' said Bee. 'They said they'd look into it, but I doubt they will.'

'Kobayashi?'

Bee shook her head. 'The museum stands to benefit significantly from Cranston's will,' she explained. 'Gus was the only thing standing between the money and Kobayashi – and she admitted that the museum was having money trouble.'

'You think she is a murderer?' Faro Costa tilted his head to the side. 'I cannot believe this. Her soul is not so dark.'

'I don't know,' said Bee. 'I still feel Cranston must be involved somehow. That's why I need to find out more. If I have more evidence, then I can take it to the police and they'll listen. But everything so far is just circumstantial. Will you help us?'

Faro Costa finished his cigarette and ground it out under his shoe. 'Very well,' he said finally. 'I will tell you all I know.'

'Thank you,' said Bee.

Faro gazed off into the distance, thinking. 'The night it happened,' he said, 'I saw nothing. I started at six o'clock in the evening. I saw nothing strange. I noticed no shadows gathering. I saw Adrian Featherstone go into his office at seven o'clock. He left just after eleven and he did not leave his office until then. The Museum Director also worked late, as did the two of you. I did not know about Gus until I was telephoned by the police the next day. The guard on duty after me found the body in the morning, when he opened the doors of the Red Rotunda.'

'So what were you doing at the time Gus died?' asked Bee. 'The police said it was around midnight.'

'I was in the control room,' said Faro. 'I make rounds every two hours, so I finished one at eleven-thirty and then made a cup of coffee and sat in the control room reading the newspaper.' He smiled. 'I like the cryptic crossword. I did not go out again until half past one.'

'What do you do in the control room?' asked Toby. 'Are there security cameras to monitor?'

Faro nodded. 'But here is a secret,' he said. 'There is no security camera in the Red Rotunda at the moment – it is faulty. So instead we lock the doors every night when the museum closes. We have the only key, so it is all safe.'

Bee raised her eyebrows. 'So anything could have happened in there,' she said. 'And you wouldn't have known.'

'Perhaps,' said Faro. 'But I do not know how anyone could have got in without the key.'

'And you definitely had the key with you the whole time?'

'I did. There is a book where people must sign the keys in and out.'

Bee glanced at Toby. 'Can we see the book?'

'You can,' said Faro. 'I can show you now; my shift is beginning.'

They went downstairs to the control room, and Faro clocked on, put on his security hat, opened a drawer and pulled out a spiral-bound exercise book.

'Here,' he said, scanning the pages. 'The Red Rotunda key was last signed out on the sixth of January, which was a week before Gus...' He paused and looked more closely at the book. 'Oh.'

'What is it?' asked Bee, leaning forward.

Faro held out the book and pointed. Under the 'Red Rotunda' column were a series of dates, names and signatures.

'What?' asked Toby from behind Bee. 'What does it say?'

Bee turned to him. 'The last person to sign out the key to the Red Rotunda was Gus, a week before he died.'

'I was here when he came to collect it,' said Faro slowly. 'He said the stuffed dog in the Red Rotunda had lost an eye and he needed to replace it.'

Bee felt as though someone had kicked her in the gut. 'That's why he had glass eyes in his pocket,' she said, half to herself. 'Oh God.'

Gus *had* killed himself. He'd been the last person to have the key to the Red Rotunda – he could have easily had a copy made before returning it. And that was why he had a pocketful of glass eyes. Because he needed the right size and shape to replace the mangy old dog's eye.

Bee swallowed. 'I'm so sorry,' she said hoarsely. 'I've made a terrible mistake.'

She thought she'd known Gus. She thought they'd shared an understanding. Gus was like her – he liked things methodical and ordered and quiet and unemotional. But was it possible that what Bee had always seen as companionable silence had actually been miserable silence? Had Gus been depressed?

'No,' said Toby. 'Bee. *No.* What about the noise we heard in the lab? Gus's fake name? The photo of Cranston

133

in Featherstone's office? And who worries about replacing a dead animal's eye on the day they're planning to top themself?'

Bee shook her head. 'I'm sure there's a rational explanation for everything,' she said, hoping she wouldn't cry in front of him.

Toby turned to Faro Costa, who was staring at the book, brow furrowed, as if he were trying to remember something. 'Who has access to the glass cases?' he asked. 'Is there a separate set of keys?'

'The display cases in the Red Rotunda have their own unique set of keys,' said Faro. 'The cases were part of the Cranston Collection. They're attached to the same keyring as the key to the door.'

'But what about the other cases?' asked Toby. 'In the rest of the museum?'

'There is one key,' said Faro. 'It opens every case in the museum, except for the ones in the Red Rotunda.' He flipped the pages of the spiral-bound book. 'And nobody has taken that key out since before Christmas.'

'And nobody else has a copy of the key?'

'Adrian Featherstone has one,' said Faro. 'His team do regular humidity checks inside the cases.'

Bee felt her heart start to hammer. 'Featherstone?' she said, weakly.

Faro nodded. 'He is a strange man, a dark man. His soul is black. He walks in shadow.' He touched the pendant hanging around his neck.

'Have you noticed anything particularly creepy about him lately?' asked Toby. 'Anything that we might be able to connect with Gus's death?'

Faro thought about it. 'Ye-es,' he said slowly. 'I did see him. Last week, in the Red Rotunda. Five days before Gus died.'

Bee tried to calm her breathing.

'Nobody else was there,' said Faro. 'Just Featherstone. And he was...*muttering*. As though he was talking to the devil himself.'

'Could you hear him?' asked Toby. 'What did he say?'

Faro scratched his head. 'He was leaning over one of the cases in there,' he said. 'I could not hear what he was muttering, so I stepped into the room to see if he was all right. And I heard him say—'

'What?' asked Toby. 'What did he say?'

'He said *It's got to be here somewhere*. Then he banged his fist on the case and turned to leave. That was when he saw me.'

'Did he say anything else?'

'No. He looked at me with eyes that burned, then he fled. I fear for him.'

'What case was Featherstone looking at?' asked Bee suddenly.

Faro Costa pursed his lips. 'The one at the front,' he said. 'The low one, with the scorpion and that strange crab.'

'Are you sure?' said Toby, suddenly sounding very intense. 'He was looking at the horseshoe crab?'

'I am sure.'

Bee's mind started to race, and she felt sick. She could barely keep up with her own emotions. Perhaps Gus hadn't killed himself. Perhaps her hunch had been right all along. Surely Featherstone had to be involved somehow? And what about Cranston?

'One last question,' she said, digging through her handbag until she found the photocopy she'd made of the newspaper article about Cranston. She handed it to Faro Costa. 'This man has been visiting the museum recently. Have you seen him?' She pointed at the photo of Cranston.

Faro squinted at the photocopy. '*Idios mío!*' he breathed. 'Yes. I have seen him many times. I saw him on the same night that I saw Featherstone in the Red Rotunda. He was around the side of the museum, near the bins. He was talking to Gus.'

'To Gus?' said Toby. 'Cranston was talking to Gus? What did he say?'

Faro shook his head. 'I did not hear,' he said. 'I only noticed them from the window of the Rainforest Exhibit. But Gus was yelling at this man. He looked...not angry, but forceful. As if he was trying to make this man do something he did not want to do.' He pointed at the picture of Cranston. 'And this man was crying.'

'Wow,' SAID TOBY, AS THEY walked up the stairs from Security. 'That was...interesting.'

'It certainly was,' said Bee.

'Can we recap?' asked Toby. 'I don't know if I got my head around it all.'

Bee nodded. 'There's no security footage of what happened in the Red Rotunda,' she said. 'And the only way to get in is with the key. The only people who have had access to the key are Faro Costa, and Gus, who had it a week earlier.'

'But he could have made a copy.'

'Exactly. Which makes the suicide explanation more likely,' said Bee. 'But I still don't buy it.'

'What about Faro Costa himself?' asked Toby. 'Should we consider him a suspect?'

Bee thought about it. 'I don't think so. He has absolutely

no motive, and he just doesn't…seem like a murderer. You know?'

Toby shrugged. 'I'm not sure anyone seems like a murderer.'

'I suppose,' said Bee.

'So what else did we learn?'

'We learnt that Cranston and Gus were seen talking a week before the murder. Gus seemed angry and Cranston was upset.'

'That doesn't really make sense,' said Toby. 'Not if Cranston is the murderer. Shouldn't *he* be the angry one? If he was threatening Gus or something?'

'Who knows? Maybe Cranston was upset that Gus wanted to work here instead of with him. Jealousy is a powerful motivation.' Bee remembered seeing Cranston in the museum the morning before Gus's death. He'd looked so *sad*. Not like the kind of man who would kill someone out of jealousy.

'And what about Featherstone?'

'Featherstone seems to have an alibi,' said Bee. 'He was seen leaving the museum just after eleven, at least an hour before the murder.'

'But he's the only one who could have opened the case with the mercuric chloride,' said Toby. 'And Faro Costa saw him in the Red Rotunda. Looking at the horseshoe crab.'

'Yes,' said Bee, chewing her lower lip. 'Why don't we stop by the Red Rotunda in case inspiration strikes?'

The Red Rotunda was as deserted as ever. Bee peered in the glass case at the horseshoe crab. 'What are your secrets?' she muttered to it. 'What have you seen in here?'

The horseshoe crab ignored her, while the scorpion next to it just looked angry.

'Bee,' said Toby. He was over by the case containing the mangy stuffed dog and cats. 'Look.'

He pointed at the dog. 'Gus said he had to replace the dog's eyes, because one of them had fallen out. But look.'

Both of the dog's eyes were there, and they were exactly the same: scratched and dull and covered in a fine layer of dust. Clearly neither had been replaced recently.

'Reptile eyes,' said Bee, suddenly.

Toby looked at her questioningly.

'The policeman said that the eyes in Gus's pocket were reptile eyes. So they couldn't have been for the dog.'

'Could Faro Costa have misheard?' asked Toby. 'Or remembered it wrong?'

'Maybe,' said Bee. 'But he doesn't seem like the kind of person who forgets things. But let's check all the eyes in here anyway. Just to make sure.'

They spent a good ten minutes examining every stuffed creature in the Red Rotunda. Bee studied the furry face of a quokka, feeling quite unsettled by all the staring glass eyes around her.

'Pull yourself together,' she whispered to herself.

'What?' asked Toby.

'Nothing,' said Bee.

'Come and look at these,' said Toby, staring into a glass case full of frogs and toads.

'Did you find anything?' asked Bee.

'Not really,' said Toby. 'Well, no, not at all. But these two toads are awesome and I want to tell you about them.'

Bee sighed and went to look at the toads.

'See this one?' Toby pointed at a flat, brown, ugly toad. 'It's called the Surinam Toad. It can't attract mates by croaking like normal frogs and toads can, so it snaps a bone in its throat, making a clicking sound. The females release eggs, and then the males sort of flip over them in the water, which embeds the eggs in the female's back. The eggs sink into the skin and form little pockets, like blisters, and then the female carries them around, right through the whole tadpole stage, until they're fully formed tiny baby toads, and then the blisters pop and they swim out.'

'That's disgusting,' said Bee. 'Now, did you find anything *useful*?'

'Don't you want to hear about the other toad?'

'No. I'm already identifying enough with this one, what with carrying everything around on my back. What does the male toad do after he's flipped the eggs into the lady toad? Probably runs off and spouts useless trivia instead of helping.'

Toby laughed. 'Well, it's funny you should say that.'

Bee groaned.

'Now look at this midwife toad.' Toby indicated a froggier-looking toad with brown lumps on its back. 'The female lays her eggs in a long string, and the male fertilises them externally. Then she vanishes, off to go shopping or drink Cosmopolitans with her girlfriends.' Toby grinned and waggled his eyebrows at Bee. 'The male toad wraps the strand of eggs around his back legs, and then swims off with them. He's got little poison sacs on his back to protect them, and he carries them around like that until they hatch. That's some pretty dedicated paternal parenting.'

'Yes, yes,' said Bee. 'Very nicely played. Now let's look at eyes.'

'There's nothing here that looks new,' said Toby. 'Everything's dusty and old. That means Gus must have lied about why he needed the key.'

'Then what *were* the eyes in his pocket for?'

'If you kids need something to do,' said a voice behind them, 'I'm sure I could find something in Conservation to keep you occupied.'

Adrian Featherstone was standing in the doorway of the Red Rotunda, holding a small cardboard box and a clipboard. He was wearing an ill-fitting white dress shirt with the buttons done up wrong, high-waisted jeans and open-toed sandals. His hair was greasy, and he looked as if he hadn't slept in a week.

'Sorry, Adrian,' said Toby, with the easy grin that seemed to make most people comfortable. 'We were just taking a quick break. It can get pretty stuffy down in the lab.'

The easy grin didn't achieve its desired effect on Featherstone. Bee had a sudden flashback to Monday morning, when she had come across Featherstone sitting at Gus's desk, scowling just like that, and rolling a glass eye between his fingers. A glass eye that Bee had guessed was a size 4...

'A reptile eye,' she said out loud before she could stop herself.

Featherstone looked at her sharply. 'I beg your pardon?'

Adrian Featherstone had been seen acting suspiciously in the Red Rotunda. Adrian Featherstone had been the last person to open the case containing the mercuric chloride. Adrian Featherstone had almost certainly been searching Gus's desk on Monday. Adrian Featherstone had been holding a glass lizard's eye that was *the same kind* as the ones found in Gus's pocket.

'Actually,' said Toby suddenly, 'that would be awesome.'

Bee and Featherstone both stared at him. 'What?' said Featherstone.

'It does get really stuffy in the taxidermy lab. And I've always been interested in conservation. We'd love to help out in your department for a couple of hours...see how it all works.'

Bee had not thought it possible for Featherstone to look *more* sour, but it seemed Toby's words had achieved it. 'Fine,' he said shortly, and stalked out of the room. Bee scurried after him with Toby trailing behind her.

'What are you *doing*?' hissed Bee. 'You don't want to know more about conservation! You said yesterday how terrified you were around all those pregnant women.'

'I want to know more about *him*,' whispered Toby, leaning in so his breath tickled Bee's ear and made her tingle inside. 'You said yourself he's involved in this. We need to find out how.'

☾ ☾ ☾

The Conservation lab was blinding, all white walls and stainless steel benches. A heavily pregnant woman gave Bee and Toby a stern glance before stripping off her latex gloves at one of the many handwashing stations, and pumping anti-bacterial handwash into her palm. She washed carefully from just above her wrist, giving each fingernail special attention, before drying her hands on a disposable towel, picking up a cardboard archive box, and stalking out of the room. Bee wasn't sure who the conservator disapproved of more: her and Toby, or the sloppy untidiness of Adrian Featherstone.

'Do you know what the word *entropy* means?' asked Featherstone. The harsh fluorescent lights showed up the pockmarks in his skin. He clearly hadn't shaved for a few days.

Bee shook her head.

'Isn't it something to do with thermodynamics?' asked Toby.

'Yes,' Featherstone said testily. 'It comes from the Greek *entropia*, which means *a turning*. And it *is* used in thermodynamics.' His face assumed its usual air of condescension. 'But more broadly it refers to the tendency of things, when left to themselves, to descend into chaos.'

Bee and Toby exchanged a glance.

'Everything,' Featherstone continued, 'regardless of whether it is natural or manufactured by humans, is in a constant state of decay. From the day you are born, you start to die. Some things simply take longer than others.'

Bee thought of Gus and shivered.

'Decay is unavoidable. Every piece of wood is rotting. Every piece of metal is rusting. Every stone is eroding. Every living creature takes a step closer to death with every breath and heartbeat. Nothing can be done to stop this. There is no way to cheat death.'

'Cheery,' remarked Toby. 'Do you give this speech to all the work-experience kids?'

Adrian Featherstone ignored him. 'My job,' he went on, 'is not to prevent entropy. It cannot be halted. My job is to control it. To limit decay.'

'You're a hero,' said Toby under his breath.

'You're obviously very good at your job,' said Bee, trying to seem friendly. 'Very passionate.'

'Yeah,' said Toby. 'Have you always been a conservationist?'

'A *conservationist*,' Featherstone said icily, 'is a kind of hippy. People who work here are *conservators*. But I am a *scientist*.'

'So how can we help you today?' asked Bee, shooting a warning glare at Toby to behave.

146

'We've recently received a shipment of preserved animals that are to be part of the upcoming new exhibition,' said Featherstone, looking bored. 'They're from a museum in Canberra, and some of the specimens are over a hundred years old. This means they're riddled with bugs and dangerous chemicals such as arsenic, DDT and mercury.'

Bee's ears pricked up. Gus had been killed using a form of mercury.

'It's our job to strip the specimens of their unwanted chemicals and creatures, and then restore them to exhibition standard.'

'Great,' said Bee. 'Where do we start?'

'The specimens are very valuable and fragile,' said Featherstone. 'They can only be handled by trained professionals. You will be inputting the notes from our conservators into our online database.'

'Data entry?' said Toby, crestfallen.

'Records and observations are vital components of preservation and conservation,' snapped Featherstone. 'As I said before, we work hard here. Don't expect me to mollycoddle you the way Gus did.'

Bee bit back a sharp retort. Sniping at Featherstone wasn't going to bring Gus back, or help them find out who killed him. She remembered the newspaper clipping that had been in Featherstone's office. He knew that Gus was really Gregory Uriel Swindon. He knew about his connection with William Cranston. But what *else* did Featherstone know?

Toby was clearly thinking along similar lines, because he turned to Featherstone with a casual air. 'So you haven't worked in science since you left England?'

Featherstone bristled. 'Conservation *is* a science,' he said stiffly. 'And you shouldn't be so quick to assume knowledge about someone from their accent. For all you know, I could have lived here since I was a boy.'

His expression suggested that the thought of living in Australia since childhood was utterly repulsive to him.

'Of course,' murmured Toby. 'Sorry.'

Featherstone installed them at adjacent workstations and curtly demonstrated how to input the information on each card into the online database. Then he stood ostentatiously over them and watched as Bee worked her way through the first card.

'I think we've got it, thanks, Adrian,' said Toby.

Adrian Featherstone raised his eyebrows and indicated that Bee should move on to the next card. Toby sighed.

There was a click of heels behind them, and they turned to see Akiko Kobayashi standing in the doorway. She looked startled to see Bee and Toby, and Bee thought she detected the faintest rosy blush on her cheeks.

'Adrian,' said Kobayashi, 'I wanted to talk to you about the...meeting. At the...department.'

Featherstone practically ran across the room to where she was standing. 'Yes,' he said. 'Yes, yes. The meeting. At the department. Yes. Let's discuss it in my office.'

He ushered Kobayashi out of the lab, leaving Bee and Toby alone. Bee replayed the last few moments in her head. There was something...odd about the way Kobayashi and Featherstone spoke to each other. Could they be having an affair?

'*Surely* it was him,' said Toby softly. 'Did you hear him going on about death and decay?'

An affair was impossible, Bee concluded. Kobayashi was beautiful and immaculately presented, and Featherstone was a giant creep. There was no way she'd ever go for him. She dismissed the thought, and told Toby about Featherstone fiddling with a glass lizard eye in the taxidermy lab.

'What kind of lizard eye?' asked Toby. 'Was the pupil a slit? Or round?'

'Slit,' said Bee. 'Why do you ask?'

'Reptiles with a slit pupil are usually venomous,' he said. 'Round pupil indicates they're not dangerous.'

'Useful.'

Toby shrugged. 'Generally if you're close enough to a snake to see the shape of his pupils, you're already in trouble.'

'I suppose. Anyway, it's not like the snake or lizard that the eyes were for was still poisonous.'

'Venomous,' corrected Toby. 'Snakes aren't poisonous. They're venomous. And the venom remains active after the snake is dead, if it's kept under the right conditions.'

'What's the difference?'

'Poison is ingested,' said Toby. 'Venom is injected. You can drink snake venom and it won't harm you at all. It has to pierce your skin and enter your bloodstream. There are only two poisonous snakes, the Japanese grass snake and the common garter snake. And they're only poisonous because they eat other things that are poisonous. Such as toads.'

Bee made a face.

'Either way,' said Toby, 'there's nothing venomous about snake or lizard eyes. Especially glass ones.'

'But they're still important,' said Bee. 'I *know* it.'

'It totally points towards Featherstone as our key suspect, right?'

Bee thought about it. 'I don't know, I still think we're missing something.'

'What kind of something?'

Bee shook her head. 'Not sure,' she said. 'Not something really big. I just feel that there's a detail I'm overlooking. Something that's going to make all these knots unravel.' She clenched her hand into a fist. 'I *wish* I could talk to Cranston! I'm *sure* I'd figure it out then.'

Toby didn't reply. Bee flicked through the pile of cards they were supposed to be entering into the database.

'You know,' said Toby, as he gazed distastefully at the computer screen, 'plenty of animals are immune to snake-bites. The mongoose. Honey badger. Secretary bird. Hedgehog. Also maybe the pig and the garden dormouse. And there are some groups of Californian ground squirrel that are immune to rattlesnake venom.'

Bee tried not to think about whether Celestial Badgers, as well as honey badgers, were immune to snakebites.

'Sorry,' said Toby. 'Not really relevant.'

Bee shook her head, and compiled a mental list of questions.

- Why had Featherstone been going through Gus's drawer the other day?
- Why had he had a lizard's eye in his hand?
- Why did he have the newspaper clipping about Gus and Cranston?

- And if he'd known Gus's true identity, why hadn't he said anything?
- Had it been Featherstone who'd taken the mercuric chloride from the display case?
- What had he been looking for when Faro Costa had seen him in the Red Rotunda?

Bee frowned. Who *was* Adrian Featherstone? His shabby, sloppy figure seemed so out of place in the Conservation labs, and the army of severe pregnant women clearly disapproved of him. Was Toby right: had he been a scientist in England before he'd come to the museum? Had he known Cranston and Gus before he came here? How did he even *get* a job as a conservator, if it wasn't his speciality? Why did Kobayashi act so strangely around him? Maybe they *were* having an affair, and that's how he got the job.

'Come on,' she said to Toby. 'Let's get out of here.'

'But what about these?' He indicated the pile of cards.

'Just leave them,' she said. 'We're not going to find out anything else here, and I'll be damned if I'm doing the conservators' admin for them. We've got enough work of our own to get on with.'

They made their way back to the preparatory studios in silence, Bee still trying to dredge that elusive key to the clues from the corners of her mind.

As they passed the maceration lab, Toby pointed at a large cupboard off a recess in the hallway. 'What's in there?'

Bee looked where he was pointing. There was a sign on the cupboard door that said HOTEL BUGGIATO in blue biro. 'Beetles.'

'As in "A Hard Day's Night"?'

'As in dung. They're dermestid beetles.'

She opened the door and a waft of warm air came out, along with a stench of decaying flesh.

'Ew,' said Toby. 'You mean like a carpet beetle? But they're not interesting at all. Are they for the Invertebrate Exhibit?'

He peered into the cupboard, which was very dimly lit by a low-wattage bulb covered in brown cellophane. 'Are they *moving*? I thought there was a special department for live exhibits?'

'They're not for an exhibit,' said Bee. 'They're for cleaning skeletons.'

'We have *flesh-eating beetles*? In a *cupboard*?'

'Some animals are too fragile for the maceration tank. They have such tiny delicate bones that they'll just get lost. This is a better way of doing it.'

'But they only eat dead flesh, right?'

'Yep. So they could probably give you a nice pedicure, like those fish you read about.'

'*Garra rufa*,' said Toby. 'Or doctor fish. They're originally from Turkey.'

Bee glanced at him sideways. 'How is it that you know everything's fancy Latin name, but nothing about what they're actually *for*?'

'It's my unique study method,' replied Toby.

'Which is?'

'Wikipedia.'

'Naturally,' said Bee. 'Heaven forbid you should actually crack a book and learn something *useful*.'

'I know, right?' said Toby. 'Kids today. Newfangled technology. Disgusting. So tell me more about these flesh-eating beetles.'

'They're pretty picky. Sometimes they won't eat whatever we put in there, so we have to spray it with Vegemite and beer.'

'Vegemite and beer.'

Bee grinned. 'They're good Australian beetles.'

As Bee walked through the doors of the museum on Friday morning, she wondered if she was making a giant mistake. It was one week exactly since she'd learned of Gus's death. Was she crazy, looking for a murderer who didn't exist? Could Adrian Featherstone really be a killer?

She supervised Toby while he skinned the partially thawed koala, and finished off the last few details on two of Gus's projects. Then she and Toby trooped upstairs to the museum's café for lunch.

Bee ordered a gourmet meat pie, and Toby asked for a ham and salad baguette with no beetroot.

'They're premade,' said the woman behind the counter. 'No special orders.'

Toby smiled charmingly at her. 'Have you changed your hair? You're looking smashing.'

155

She rolled her eyes, but blushed and sliced open a fresh bread roll.

They took a number for their table and sat by the window. A couple sat nearby holding hands and staring gooily at each other over a vanilla slice. Bee gritted her teeth. Fletch had never looked at her like that. Nobody had ever looked at her like that. Not that she wanted Fletch to look at her that way – the thought made her feel uncomfortable somehow. A sudden vision flashed in front of her, of Toby holding her hand and gazing into her eyes. She shook her head to dislodge the vision. She was crazy.

'Don't you love the way that all cafés smell the same?' asked Toby. 'Whether it's a school or hospital or museum. Whether a ham and salad roll costs three-fifty or twelve dollars and comes with garnish.'

'Yeah,' said Bee, ripping open a sugar packet and letting the little white grains trickle onto the tabletop.

'Are you okay?'

Bee nodded and trailed her finger in the sugar, swirling it into different shapes.

A waitress brought over a pie and a baguette on white plates.

'Sauce?' she asked Bee.

'Yes, please.'

The waitress took away the number and returned with a tomato-shaped squeezy sauce bottle.

'Classy,' said Toby. 'You're lucky they didn't charge you an extra twelve dollars for it.'

Bee stared at her pie.

'You're sure you're okay?' asked Toby again, lifting a decorative sprig of curly parsley from the edge of his plate with a look of distaste.

'I still feel like I'm missing something,' said Bee. 'Something to do with Gus. Obviously.'

'I'm sure it'll come to you,' said Toby, biting into his salad roll.

'I hope so,' said Bee. She picked up the tomato sauce and splodged some onto the pie. Then she frowned and narrowed her eyes, making the red blob go all fuzzy.

'Wait,' she murmured. 'It's almost there.' She looked up at Toby. 'What did you say?'

'I didn't say anything,' he said, his mouth full.

'No,' said Bee. 'Before. What did you say to the lady behind the counter?'

'I asked her if she'd changed her hair.'

'Before that.'

'Can I have a ham and salad baguette?'

Bee snapped her fingers. 'Beetroot.'

'What?'

'You asked for *no beetroot.*'

'Yeah,' said Toby. 'I don't like the way it gets into all the other ingredients. It's like the George Lucas of salad vegetables. It turns once-fine vegetables into soggy pink nonsense.'

Bee had a flashback to Gus eating a salad sandwich on the day of his death. She saw the beetroot sliding out the bottom of the sandwich and falling onto his hoodie.

His green museum hoodie. All the staff were given a hoodie to help combat the chill from the museum's regulated temperature. But most people thought they were daggy and didn't wear them. Except...

'Toby,' she said quickly. 'Think back to when they found Gus in the Red Rotunda. When we saw him. Can you remember if there was a stain on his hoodie?'

Toby blinked. 'I don't remember noticing one,' he said. 'But my mind was on other things, like, oh look, there's a dead guy on the floor.'

'We have to go back to Conservation,' Bee said. 'And I need you to get Featherstone out of his office for five minutes so I can go in and check something.'

'Easy,' said Toby, and stood up. 'Wait here for two minutes, then go down.'

He walked briskly out of the café.

Bee waited, and then made her way to Adrian Featherstone's office. She earned glares from three pregnant women, but smiled sunnily and told them Featherstone had sent her to collect a folder. She knocked softly on his office door, and when nobody answered, she slipped inside and closed the door behind her. She picked her way through the debris until she found what she was looking for: a green museum hoodie, tangled in the wheels of Featherstone's desk chair. She untangled it and held it up.

There was a faint, pinkish-purple stain on the front.

Why did Adrian Featherstone have Gus's hoodie? Did that mean that Gus had been found dead in Featherstone's hoodie? If so, did the glass eyes belong to Featherstone?

Bee ran a finger over the stain. This complicated things somewhat. It certainly implicated Featherstone – he'd obviously had contact with Gus on his last day, enough contact for their clothes to be swapped around. But there were a million reasons why Adrian Featherstone might have glass eyes in his pocket, and most of them were entirely legitimate. But what if the eyes *were* some kind of vital clue?

It was just the kind of evidence to be found in a Miss Marple mystery. A pocketful of eyes. It spoke of mystery and intrigue and devilish plotting. It could have been the signature of a serial killer...or it could have been Gus's last desperate attempt to explain who his killer was.

But, as Bee kept having to remind herself, real life wasn't a Miss Marple mystery. The point was, even if the eyes themselves weren't a clue, they must belong to Featherstone. So why had Gus been wearing Featherstone's hoodie when he died?

Bee heard a telephone ringing outside, and sprang to her feet. Eyes were irrelevant. She didn't want to be caught snooping around Featherstone's office. She dropped the hoodie back on the floor and quickly made her way back to the taxidermy lab.

A few minutes later, Toby joined her.

'Thanks,' she said. 'How did you get rid of him?'

He grinned. 'I had a problem with the computer,' he said. 'The one I was inputting all that data on.'

'What kind of a problem?'

Toby held up a power cord. 'I don't know,' he said, wide-eyed and shrugging. 'It just turned off, all by itself. I couldn't figure out what had happened. I left Featherstone on the phone to the IT department.'

'Good work.'

'So did you find what you were looking for?'

Bee relayed her discovery of the beetroot stain on Gus's hoodie.

'So the glass eyes were a red herring,' said Toby. 'That's a bit disappointing.'

'Not entirely,' said Bee. 'They helped lead us to Adrian Featherstone.'

'Maybe. But a Natural History Museum hoodie is not nearly so intriguing a clue as a pocketful of glass eyes.'

'A clue is still a clue.'

'I suppose. So what now?'

'We need the dirt on Featherstone,' said Bee. 'There's absolutely no doubt that he's somehow involved in Gus's death. I want to know where he came from, and what he did before he came to the museum. If conservation is "just a hobby", I want to know what his *real* job is. I want to know what he has for breakfast every morning.'

'Great,' said Toby. 'A research mission. What are you doing Saturday?'

Bee made a face. 'I have to go on some kind of torturous outing with my mum and the Celestial Badger.'

'He isn't really a badger, is he?'

'Sadly, no,' said Bee. 'I kind of think it would be better if he was. He's an accountant.'

'Oh.' Toby looked disappointed.

'I don't want to go,' said Bee. 'How am I supposed to behave around my mum's new badger boyfriend? Am I supposed to *bond* with him?'

Toby shrugged. 'I recommend you line your shoes with eggshells.'

'I beg your pardon?'

'It's a Scandinavian thing,' said Toby in an infuriatingly offhand manner. 'They put eggshells in their boots when they're entering badger territory. Those little buggers have specially wired jaws that mean when they bite you, they *never* let go until the bones are broken. So they tend to hold on until they hear a *crunch*. Hence the eggshells. I wouldn't want your mum's new boyfriend to bite off your foot. Wouldn't really be a good start for what I'm sure will be a beautiful friendship.'

Bee scowled at him. 'I suppose you're a goldmine of useless badger trivia.'

'Maybe. Maybe I know that badger meat is a popular ingredient in the Russian shish kabob.'

'Why did I ask?' Bee shook her head. 'I wish I could get out of it, but I promised. Mum's trying to be all Happy Families.'

Toby grinned. 'Leave it to me,' he said. 'I've got a hunch I know where to look to find out all about Featherstone. I'll call you on the weekend if I find anything.'

He waved and strode off toward the train station. Bee sighed. A goodbye hug might have been nice.

She noticed Faro Costa smoking a cigarette by the bins. He nodded at her as she approached.

'You are still in shadow,' he said. 'You must learn to turn your face to the sun.'

Bee smiled at him. 'I will, I promise. But do you think you could help me? I'm trying to learn more about Featherstone. Can you tell me exactly when you saw him on the day Gus died?'

Faro thought about it. 'Well, he was away from the museum for most of the day. He came back at seven, checked the new exhibition space and then went to his office and stayed there until eleven when he left. I did not see him after that until my next shift, which was the next night.'

'And he definitely left the building?' asked Bee. 'And didn't come back?'

Faro nodded. 'There is a special alert for anyone who enters the building after closing,' he said. 'And nobody did.'

'And you never saw Gus enter or leave the building?' Bee demanded.

'I did not see him.'

'So Gus was here the whole time,' she said. 'I wonder where he went after he left the lab.'

'I hope you will find out the answer to your puzzle,' said Faro. 'So that you can come out of the shadow, and so Gus's spirit can be at peace. I fear he is trapped here until the answer is found.'

'I just wish I could talk to Cranston,' Bee muttered. 'I'm sure it'd all fall into place.'

'Cranston? The man in the photo you showed me? The man I saw with Gus? The man who cried?'

Bee nodded.

'Why don't you talk to him?' asked Faro.

'I can't *find* him.'

Faro looked confused. 'He is over there.' He pointed.

Bee turned. Faro Costa was right. William Cranston was sitting on a park bench near the entrance to the museum, in exactly the same place she'd seen him the morning after Gus's death.

'He is there often,' said Faro. 'He reads the newspaper and feeds crumbs to the birds.'

Bee opened her mouth to say something, and then started to laugh.

'Did I say a funny joke?' said Faro Costa.

'No,' said Bee. 'But I guess you were right. I did need to come out of the shadows into the light. What I was looking for was out here all along. Thank you.'

Faro Costa ducked his head in acknowledgement, and lit up another cigarette.

'Excuse me,' said Bee. 'Dr Cranston?'

The old man looked up, startled. Bee hesitated, disconcerted by those pale blue eyes, then shook her head and introduced herself.

'I worked with Gus,' she said. 'I just... I wanted to talk to you about him. I promise I won't disturb you for long.'

Cranston seemed uncomfortable. 'Why would you want to talk to me?' he asked. His British accent wasn't posh and plummy like Adrian Featherstone's, but rather rougher and growlier – the accent of someone who had to work for a living.

'I know that Gus was really Gregory Uriel Swindon,' she explained. 'I know he used to work for you.'

Cranston's pale blue eyes were sharp and alert. He might be old, but he was certainly in full control of his mind. For a moment, Bee thought he was going to say something, but he just looked concerned.

'Please,' she said. 'I'd really like to know more about him.'

The deep lines of Cranston's face drooped, and Bee thought she had never seen anyone look so sad.

'He was...a loyal employee,' he said at last. 'And a good friend.'

Bee shook her head. 'So why would he kill himself?' she asked. 'Can you think of any possible reason?'

Cranston was silent for a long time, gazing into the distance. Bee wanted desperately to know what he was thinking, what memories were passing before his eyes.

'I'm sorry,' said Cranston at last. 'I can't help you. Gus hadn't been a member of my staff for some time before he died. I hadn't seen him for several years.'

Bee opened her mouth to tell him that she knew this to be a lie, but changed her mind. 'Why did he stop working for you? Did you have a falling-out?'

'Gregory had been in my employ for over forty years,' said Cranston. 'He was an old man, older than me. He deserved a long and happy retirement.'

'So why go back to work? And why doing taxidermy at the museum?'

Cranston's smile made Bee's heart break a little. 'I think he was only happy when he was working,' he said. 'Neither of us had any family left. And taxidermy was always his hobby. We used to joke about it – I spent my whole career taking creatures apart to study their workings, and Gregory put them back together again.'

'And you don't have any idea why he might have wanted to kill himself?'

William Cranston shook his head. 'I don't know,' he said. 'I just don't know.' He stood up. 'I'm very sorry I couldn't help you more, but I must be leaving.'

'Just one more thing before you go,' Bee said. 'Does the name Adrian Featherstone mean anything to you?'

A dark cloud passed over William Cranston's face. 'No,' he said shortly. 'The name means nothing.'

He tucked his paper under his arm and hurried away. Bee watched him go. Had he told her the truth about anything at all?

13

IF BEE WERE TO MAKE a list of the ten things that made her the most uncomfortable, they would have included:

1. Luna Park.
2. Rides where she had to go upside down.
3. Seeing her mother goggle dopily at a scrawny, pudding-bowl-haired guy (who moonlighted as a Celestial Badger) as though he was Robert Downey Jnr.
4. Watching the aforementioned Celestial Badger attempt to throw balls in the mouths of clowns in order to win a stuffed animal for her mother, and fail miserably.
5. The feeling of a slightly undercooked hotdog, hard and rocklike, in her belly.

6. The combination of an upside-down ride and an undercooked hotdog, with the addition of a large blue milkshake.
7. Being sick in a public toilet.
8. Trying to hide the fact that she was nauseous from her mother, because she didn't want to spoil Angela's Fun Happy Family Outing.
9. Having tomato sauce smeared on her by a feral screaming child.
10. The dentist.

The day's entertainment had so far ticked boxes 1–9, and, judging by the amount of sugar in the large blue milkshake, a visit to the dentist was certainly on the cards.

'So,' said Angela, plonking herself onto the seat beside Bee. 'What ride shall we go on next?' She grinned at the Celestial Badger, who pulled something lumpy out of his pocket. Bee tried to look enthusiastic as Angela tossed the twenty-sided die carefully onto the ground.

'Fourteen,' said Angela, looking at her map of Luna Park. 'That's the G-Force.'

Bee shuddered at the thought of being violently spun around.

'But it's minus three because we just had those milk-shakes,' said the Badger. 'So it's eleven.'

Angela screwed up her nose. 'But we've already been on the Pharaoh's Curse twice.'

'Then let's add two because we gained XP on the Shock Drop. Then it's the Scenic Railway.' The Badger looked pleased. 'That's the biggest ride here, so we should get extra XP for it.'

Angela nodded. 'But let's get popcorn first.' She grinned. 'Initiative check!'

She rolled the die and got a three. 'Awesome. And my dexterity modifier of plus three still only makes a six.'

Bee shook her head through a haze of nausea and blue milkshake. 'Don't you want it to be higher?'

'Usually,' said Angela. 'But we're deciding who has to get the popcorn.'

The Celestial Badger rolled the die and got a five.

'Hah!' said Angela. 'You have a dexterity modifier of *two*, so it's popcorn time for you!'

'But I'm flat-footed,' he replied with a grin. 'So I don't get any dexterity modifier. That means I'm just a five. You win.'

'You are *not* flat-footed,' said Angela. 'And even if you were, that's only for when you're surprised in combat.'

The Celestial Badger looked over at the popcorn stand. 'I expect that there will be some combat over there,' he said. 'Did you see that kid with the shaved head?'

'Even if there is combat,' said Angela, 'you still have to get over there. And you have the travel domain, so you won't be affected by spells that impede movement. And *my* movement has been affected by that hotdog I had before.'

'Ah,' said the Badger, 'but you're a Rogue Elf, which means you have uncanny dodge, and are more likely to withstand a surprise attack from shaven-headed-kid.'

Bee stood up and her stomach lurched again. 'I'll get the popcorn.'

'Thanks, love,' said Angela.

'Don't forget to check for traps,' said the Celestial Badger, suddenly very serious. 'And maybe detect magic if anything looks strange.'

Bee ignored this advice, and made her way woozily to one of the food stands, weaving through the crowds and trying not to inhale the smell from the hotdog cart. She was a little lightheaded; the noise and clamour pressed in on her, all spinning rides and flashing lights and whistles.

She wondered what Toby was doing. Was he finding information about Featherstone? Was he thinking about her? She went to check her phone for messages, but realised she'd left it on her bedside table. A mistake that Poirot never would have made.

The tacky glitz of the amusement park seemed so completely normal, Bee found it hard to imagine that her days in the cool taxidermy lab had really happened. Could Gus be dead? Surely that kind of thing didn't happen in real life. Bee walked unheedingly past a toddler throwing a major tantrum. The sun was strong and hot, and the top of Bee's head felt tight with sunburn.

The woman in front of Bee in the queue for popcorn looked a bit like Akiko Kobayashi. Bee wondered just how far Kobayashi would go to save her museum. Would she resort to murder?

A piercing cry startled Bee out of her thoughts, but it was coming from the direction of the Circus of Screams, so it was probably nothing to be concerned about.

She remembered visiting Luna Park with Fletch and Maddy last year. Fletch had insisted they go into the Circus of Screams, and Bee had wondered if it was because he wanted an opportunity to grope her in the darkness. But he hadn't even held her hand. At the time Bee had been glad – she'd liked how Fletch kept public displays of affection to an absolute minimum. Now she wondered if he'd been holding Maddy's hand instead. She imagined coming here with Toby, on a date. It might be quite nice to hold his hand in the Circus of Screams. And maybe steal a kiss or two...

Bee reached for the jumbo-sized popcorn and tasted blue milkshake in the back of her throat. The popcorn wobbled before her, and for a moment it looked like a cardboard container full of shining glass lizard eyes.

What was Featherstone up to?

Angela and the Celestial Badger weren't sitting on the bench when Bee returned. She looked around, and spotted a blob of red crushed velvet over by the Fun House.

Bee traipsed over to them. The Celestial Badger was in front of one of the wacky mirrors, which made him look all shrunken and tiny and wasted, while Angela's reflection bulged and stretched. They were both pointing and laughing so hard that tears were streaming down Angela's face. Bee rather uncharitably thought she couldn't see much difference between the reflections and the real thing.

She caught sight of her own reflection, all wavy and wobbly and insubstantial. Her distorted face was very pale, and her hair was a mess. Stupid Luna Park. Stupid undercooked hotdog. As Bee passed another mirror, her reflection disappeared entirely. Invisibility would be good. Then she could sneak into Featherstone's office and eavesdrop. She sighed. Maybe Featherstone had the ability to turn invisible. Maybe that's how he'd killed Gus.

'The wandering adventurer returns triumphant!' said the Celestial Badger, as Bee handed Angela the popcorn.

Bee ground her teeth and didn't reply. The Celestial Badger's over-friendly schtick was starting to grate on her.

Angela laughed and pointed at the mirror in front of Bee. It was a confusing warped one that crossed over with the mirror next to it, so it seemed as if the Celestial Badger's head was on Bee's body, and Bee's head was on the Badger's body. Bee made a face.

'Wow, I guess makeovers *can* work miracles!' said the Badger with a giggle. 'I feel like a whole new person! Hey Bee, I love your new haircut. It totally suits you.'

Bee said nothing. She was in a nightmare.

'Hey, you don't look so good,' said the Badger, suddenly serious. 'Are you okay?'

'I *was* fine,' snapped Bee, 'until you came along and stuck your head on mine.'

'Bee,' said Angela in a warning voice. 'Please don't speak to Neal with that tone.'

'Fine, I'll go back to not speaking to him at all.'

There was an uncomfortable pause. Angela glared.

'Bee, I'd like you to apologise to Neal.'

'Angela, it's fine—' the Badger started, but Angela shook her head.

'No, I want to hear you apologise, Bee. You're acting like a spoilt child and I know you're more mature than this.'

Bee felt sick and weary. All she wanted was to curl up in her bed away from Badgers and mirrors and glass eyes and murderers.

'I'm sorry, Neal,' she said, meeting his eye. 'I shouldn't have said those things. I'm just finding it hard to adjust to my mum having a boyfriend. It won't happen again.'

The Celestial Badger blushed. Angela nodded briskly.

'Right,' she said. 'It must be time for us to ride the Scenic Railway.'

When they arrived home that evening, Angela suggested a game of Star Wars Monopoly and a pizza.

'I'm tired,' said Bee. 'And I ate too much at Luna Park, so if it's okay I might just go to bed.'

Angela looked concerned. 'Are you sure?' she said. 'It's only seven-thirty.'

'I'm fine,' said Bee. 'Just really tired. Work has been busy. You guys have a good night.'

'Sleep well,' said the Celestial Badger with a wave.

Bee grabbed a packet of antacid tablets from the bathroom, and kicked off her shoes. She didn't bother getting undressed, just crawled into bed and pulled the blankets over her head. Her stomach was still churning from the hotdog-milkshake-upside-down combination. She wondered absently if Toby'd had any luck finding anything on Featherstone, but couldn't quite bring herself to check her phone for messages. She closed her eyes and tried to think of clear lakes and gentle breezes until eventually she drifted off to sleep.

Her phone rattled on her bedside table, startling her into wakefulness. It was nearly eleven, and the house was quiet.

She answered it groggily. It was Toby.

'Where have you been all day?' he asked. 'I've been trying to call you.'

Bee made a squeaking groaning noise. 'Luna Park. I left my phone at home.'

'Whatever,' said Toby. 'Meet me at that all-night café on Park Street in half an hour?'

'What?' said Bee, fumbling for her bedside light. 'Can't you just tell me over the phone? Or wait until Monday?'

'Come on, Bee!' said Toby. 'What kind of investigator are you? We need to exchange information in a seedy diner late at night.'

'It's not a seedy diner,' said Bee. 'It's an art gallery café that has occasional live folk music.'

'Whatever. Just be there.'

The phone clicked as Toby hung up, and Bee swung her legs over the side of her bed and tried to locate her shoes.

Toby was already there when Bee stumbled through the café door, blinking at the sudden light. She grimaced when she saw he was drinking a spearmint milkshake.

'Did you know,' said Toby, apropos of nothing, 'that people don't actually drop to the ground because of the mechanics of being shot?'

'What?'

The waitress came over and Bee queasily ordered a plain mineral water.

'It's psychological.' Toby slurped at his milkshake. 'It takes ten to twelve seconds to pass out from blood loss, so physically, you're able to stand for that long. It's your brain going *Oh no! I've been shot! I'd better drop to the ground*. When animals get shot, they just keep running. Except for dogs, who clearly watch too much *CSI*.'

'Dogs aren't the only ones.'

'Are you okay?' Toby asked, peering at Bee. 'You look dreadful.'

'Thanks. Now tell me what you found out.'

'Adrian Alice Featherstone,' said Toby. 'I can't tell you why he has a girl's middle name, but I can tell you that he is forty-nine years old. He was born in Jersey, England, boarded at Tonbridge School in Kent, and studied biology and chemistry at Cambridge University. He then went on to work for a variety of independent science laboratories, specialising in molecular biology. In 1986 he was working for BioFresh, a company that did freelance research and labwork for other scientists. Bookmark that for later. He has marmalade on toast for breakfast.'

Bee blinked. 'What? How did you find all this out?'

Toby leaned forward over the table. 'I had an interesting conversation last night with my anatomy professor, and he gave me the name of a UK database which is a directory of scientists. There's a copy of the database in the Science Library at uni. I went in today and looked up Featherstone. There was a brief bio attached to his reference.'

'Well done,' said Bee. 'And how did you find out what he eats for breakfast?'

Toby grinned. 'I made that bit up. I figure he's English, so marmalade's an educated guess.'

'So he's a molecular biologist,' said Bee. 'I wonder if that's his connection to Cranston.'

'I am *so* far ahead of you,' said Toby. 'After I found that, I did a search in all the science journals we have online at uni for William Cranston and BioFresh. And I found that he outsourced some of his research to them. In 1986.'

'What kind of research?' asked Bee.

'Horseshoe crabs.'

Bee swallowed.

'So I went back to my lecturer, and asked him for more info about the whole horseshoe crab thing. And he remembered this rumour that had been going round at the time. About why Cranston didn't get his Nobel Prize.'

Toby paused for dramatic emphasis, and Bee kicked him under the table. 'Get on with it.'

'Just before the Nobel nominations were announced, a pharmaceuticals company announced they'd made a breakthrough: a new way to test for bacteria in pharmaceuticals using haemoglobins from...'

'Horseshoe crabs,' said Bee.

'Exactly. Cranston's name was muddied and he lost his Nobel nomination. Then there was this whole brouhaha about whether he'd sold the research to the pharmaceuticals company himself, or whether one of his researchers had sold him out.' He took a sip of his milkshake, and winked at Bee. 'One more thing I found out about Adrian Featherstone and BioFresh?'

'Yes?'

'He left there in 1986,' said Toby smugly. 'And didn't turn up in any other scientific database again. The next mention I found of him was a press release from twelve months ago, when he started working at the museum.'

'It was him,' breathed Bee. 'He sold Cranston's research to the pharmaceuticals company.'

'It sure looks like it,' said Toby. 'Now, do I get some kind of prize for figuring all that out?'

Bee gave him a flat look. 'I'll pay for your milkshake,' she said.

BEE WASN'T TIRED. HER STOMACH still felt a little jangly from Luna Park, but she didn't want to sleep. She sat at her desk, opened a spiral-bound notebook and sharpened a pencil. She half-considered making a spreadsheet, but decided that it would be better done old-school. She smoothed the paper, and started to write.

SUSPECTS

GUS WHITTAKER (AKA GREGORY URIEL SWINDON)

Gus could have committed suicide.

Motive: He was seen yelling at Cranston so was clearly emotional about <u>something</u>.

Alibi: n/a

Questions:

- Why would he have done it?
- How did he get into the Red Rotunda?
- Why was he using a fake name?
- Why was he yelling at Cranston a few days before his death?
- What kind of person eats a sandwich and then necks a bottle of poison?

AKIKO KOBAYASHI

Museum Director. Has a lot to lose if she gets caught.

Motive: The museum is having money trouble. Gus was the only person standing in the way of the museum inheriting Cranston's fortune.

Alibi: Don't know. Didn't Faro Costa say she was working late that night?

Questions:

- Why does she act so weirdly around Adrian Featherstone?
- Can they be having an affair?
- Why was she so keen to let all the staff know that Gus committed suicide?

WILLIAM CRANSTON

Gus's former employer.

Motive: Unknown. Maybe related to Featherstone and the betrayal of Cranston's research? Gus was seen yelling at Cranston, and Cranston was in tears. Perhaps he was driven into a murderous rage?

Alibi: None (and seen around the scene of the crime)

Questions: How did Cranston get access to the museum, the Red Rotunda and the glass case containing the mercuric chloride?

ADRIAN FEATHERSTONE

Conducted research on William Cranston's behalf, then sold the findings to a pharmaceuticals company. In possession of Gus's hoodie. Seen acting suspiciously in the Red Rotunda.

Motive: Perhaps another swipe at Cranston? Or had Gus found out something that Featherstone didn't want anyone to know?

Alibi: Was seen leaving the building at eleven by Faro Costa.

Questions:

• What was his relationship with Gus?

• Why did he swap hoodies?

• What is he trying to hide?

Bee put down her pencil with a sigh. What was she missing?

She thought of all the dark, complicated crime novels on her bookshelf. Nancy Drew and Trixie Belden were clearly out of their league here. She needed someone from a Raymond Chandler novel, or perhaps Inspector Rebus. What would *they* do? Run a DNA test on something, no doubt. The murder weapon.

Bee picked up the pencil again and wrote *murder weapon* at the bottom of her list, and then drew a circle around it. Perhaps it was time to pay another visit to the Conservation lab.

① ① ①

'I need your help,' she said to Toby on Monday morning.

'*My* help?' asked Toby with his cheeky smirk.

'We need to talk to some people in Conservation. Not Adrian Featherstone.'

Toby nodded. 'You want me to flirt with one of those pregnant ladies.'

'Yes.'

'That's a big ask,' said Toby. 'Some might say they are uncharmable. But as I am *very* good at flirting, I'll give it a crack. As soon as you give me a promotion.'

'What?'

'I think this will prove I'm no longer a Worthy Beginner. My powers of charm can deliver some pretty impressive clues – remember when I got that file from Kobayashi? I reckon I should be bumped up to Watson-class.'

'You can be Sally Kimball,' said Bee, grudgingly.

'Who?'

'Encyclopedia Brown's sidekick.'

'Who's Encyclopedia Brown?'

Bee gave him an incredulous look. 'Go ask your good friend Wikipedia.'

'Fine,' said Toby. 'But I'll make it to Watson. You just wait and see.'

There was only one pregnant woman in the Conservation lab. She was bent over an ancient-looking shirt with a needle and thread in her white-gloved hand.

'What a picture of domesticity,' said Toby with a smile.

The woman looked up, her brow furrowed. 'What are you doing in here?'

'We wanted to ask you some questions,' said Bee. 'About Gus—'

'About being a conservator,' interrupted Toby. 'It seems like such a fascinating line of work. Can you tell us about it?'

185

The conservator looked entirely unconvinced. 'I'm quite busy,' she said. 'You should talk to Adrian if you want career advice.'

'Actually,' said Bee, 'I wanted to know about mercuric chloride.'

The conservator raised a pair of severely shaped eyebrows. 'And why would you want to know anything about that?'

Toby kicked Bee in the ankle. 'So what are you sewing there?' he asked, turning on his charming sparkles.

'It's Henry Lawson's shirt,' the conservator said. 'And it's very fragile, so if you wouldn't mind...'

This was pointless. 'Sorry for bothering you,' said Bee. 'We'd better leave you to it.'

She turned to leave, but Toby didn't make any move to follow.

'When are you due?' he asked.

The conservator blinked, then briefly rested a hand on her belly. 'April.'

Toby took a gentle step towards her. 'I hope it all goes well,' he said. 'I think you'll be a great mother.'

Bee nearly snorted.

'Aren't you worried, though?' asked Toby. 'About all the chemicals you're exposing the baby to in here?'

The conservator seemed to soften a little. Bee couldn't believe it. 'We don't use anything toxic here,' the woman replied. 'There are conservators whose job it is to strip items of all their harmful preservatives, and replace them with new, non-toxic ones. I stopped doing that once I knew I was pregnant.'

Bee leaned forward. 'So nothing on display is preserved with toxic chemicals?'

The conservator stiffened again, as if she'd forgotten that Bee was there. 'I really should be getting back to work.'

'Of course not,' said Toby to Bee, shaking his head. 'Because our conservators are some of the best in the world.' He looked at the woman. 'Right?'

She smiled at him again. 'It's part of this museum's policy. No DDT, no lead, no arsenic, no mercury.'

Toby leaned closer with his flirtiest, most charming smile. 'What about that display of old preservation materials? Those little glass bottles of chemicals?'

The conservator actually laughed. 'Them?' she said. 'They're replicas. They're full of water.'

Bee couldn't help gasping. The woman looked at her, suspicion creeping over her face. 'What exactly did you come in here wanting to know?'

'Thanks so much for your time,' said Toby. 'Good luck with the baby!'

He dragged Bee from the room, and they hurried back to the Catacombs and stared at each other for a moment.

'Told you I was good,' said Toby.

Bee ignored him. There was no way Gus could have been killed by the mercuric chloride. Someone had stolen the bottle from its case and planted it in Gus's hand. As a decoy. To hide the *real* way he'd been killed.

'So how *did* he die?' she murmured.

She started to pace the room. This changed everything. She absently picked up a seagull wing.

'Okay,' said Toby, taking the wing away from her and putting it back on a shelf. 'How's this for a theory: Featherstone stole research from Cranston twenty-five years ago, right?'

'Right.'

'And Gus was Cranston's assistant.'

'Right.'

'So what if Gus was coming after Featherstone, as revenge, but Featherstone got there first and murdered him. *Or*, Featherstone had been threatening Cranston, and killed Gus to show he was serious.'

Bee continued to pace. 'So how do you explain the fact that Featherstone wasn't in the building at the time?'

188

she asked. 'And why would Featherstone plant the fake mercuric chloride on Gus? Surely that would just throw *more* suspicion on him, as he's one of the only people with access to that case. And why would he have swapped hoodies?'

'Well,' said Toby, looking increasingly out of his depth, 'maybe Featherstone locked Gus in the Red Rotunda earlier in the evening, and administered some kind of poison that takes a few hours to work. And planting his hoodie on Gus was a message to Cranston. The glass eyes! They were the message. They were telling Cranston that he was *watching him*, and that he'd better do what Featherstone wants.'

'Which is?'

Toby shrugged. 'Money? More research to sell?'

'And what about planting the mercuric chloride on the body?'

Toby looked stumped. Bee shook her head. 'It can't be that complicated,' she said. 'Occam's razor. There *has* to be a simple explanation.'

'Why?' asked Toby. 'Not everything's simple.'

Bee picked up a pair of tweezers and examined them. 'You know, NASA spent millions of research dollars inventing a pen that could write in space. The Russians just took pencils.'

'Not true,' said Toby. 'The space pen was invented by a guy called Paul Fisher, and NASA didn't pay him to invent it. Prior to that both the Russians and Americans used pencils, but they were dangerous when the leads broke and went floating around, and they were combustible in a one-hundred per cent oxygen atmosphere, and after the fire in Apollo 1, they wanted to be carrying less stuff around that could spontaneously catch on fire.'

Bee opened her mouth to reply, but found she had nothing to say. She put down the tweezers.

Toby grinned. 'Don't try to out-nerd me, Wikipedia Brown. It can't be done.'

Bee decided she would never figure Toby out, and that it was pointless to try. 'On the other hand,' she said, 'maybe Occam's razor is the wrong way to look at it. Sherlock Holmes always said that when you've eliminated the things that are totally impossible, whatever's left over must be the truth, no matter how improbable it is.'

'So let's eliminate the impossible,' said Toby.

They thought about it for a moment. It *all* seemed impossible.

'What does Agatha Christie say?' asked Toby.

'Poirot says that it's dangerous to let your imagination run wild, because the simplest explanation is always the best one.'

'Well, then. Back to Mr Ockham and his razor of doom.'

'It just doesn't add up. The circumstances all point towards Gus killing himself, but I can't see how that's possible. It's like we've completely missed something. Something big. It doesn't make sense. If it were a book, we would already have met the murderer by now, but not figure out it's them for another hundred pages or so. But...' Bee floundered.

Toby reached out and put his hand on hers. Bee felt all the hairs on her arm stand on end.

'Agatha Christie said something else,' said Bee.

'Oh?'

'She said, "Very few of us are what we seem."' Bee looked up at Toby. He had a strange expression on his face, sort of puzzled and smiling and...something else.

'What?' She pulled her hand away, feeling suddenly cranky.

Toby shook his head and smiled some more. 'Nothing,' he said. 'I just...never mind.'

Bee glared at him. '*Anyway*, the glass eyes led us to Featherstone, but not in a conclusive he-did-it kind of way. And now we know that the missing bottle isn't a smoking gun either, because Gus *can't* have been poisoned by the mercuric chloride.'

'So we're back to square one.'

'Maybe.' Bee picked up the tweezers again and toyed with them, thinking. 'On the other hand, someone wanted it to *look* like Gus was poisoned using the mercuric chloride. So maybe whoever killed him is trying to cast suspicion on the museum staff. On Featherstone in particular. Will you *stop* looking at me like that?'

'Sorry,' said Toby. 'But you're *very* cute when you're detecting.'

And he leaned forward, cupped her chin in his hand, and kissed her very gently on the mouth. Bee's entire body suddenly felt as if it had been dunked in fire and ice, and before she knew what she was doing she was kissing Toby back. He scooted his chair right up against hers, then pulled her off and onto his lap, wrapping his arms around her waist and pulling her face down to his. Bee touched his hair, then let her fingers rest on the back of his neck, just above his collar. He made a satisfied little noise in the back of his throat and grazed his teeth against her bottom lip. Kissing Fletch had never made her feel like this. *Nothing* had ever made her feel like this.

There was a tinny explosion of noise and Toby tensed, then broke the kiss and gently slid Bee back onto her own chair. He pulled a mobile from his pocket, glanced at the number and frowned. Bee felt her cheeks growing red, and she turned her chair to face her desk, as though she didn't care that Toby had interrupted their make-out session for a phone call. The phone rang for another few seconds, then Toby answered it.

'Hi,' he said, his voice rather hoarse. 'Yes... Yes I did... I am... I'm getting more and more convinced every day.'

He moved away from her and lowered his voice. 'I know it does, but it's not like I'm making it up... This afternoon? Fine. Bye.'

The phone snapped shut. Bee turned around, trying to look unconcerned.

'Sorry,' said Toby.

'Saved by the bell,' said Bee.

Toby grinned as if nothing had happened. 'Another reference to cadavers,' he said. 'You're doing well.'

'I am?' Bee wanted to smack the smile off his face.

'In Victorian mortuaries, they had a waiting lounge for the recently deceased, because people had a phobia of being buried alive. Doctors used to go to all sorts of crazy lengths to make sure their patients were really dead.'

Bee considered coldly ignoring him, but decided he probably wouldn't notice anyway. 'Do I dare ask?'

'They'd jam needles beneath toenails, blow bugle fanfares in ears, pour boiling wax on foreheads and warm urine in mouths, put sharp pencils up noses and administer tobacco enemas.'

'Tobacco enemas?'

'Yeah. Using a weird contraption that looked a bit like bagpipes. Anyway, after all that they'd leave them for a week just to make *really really really* sure. And they'd put a bell beside each body, so they could ring it if they woke up.'

'Saved by the bell,' said Bee.

'Saved by the bell.'

There was an awkward pause, and Bee wondered if he was going to try and kiss her again. Did she want him to? She made a quick mental list.

1. YES.
2. YES.
3. YES.
4. NO, because he was clearly a playboy and anyway, what phone call was so important that you stopped kissing a cute girl?
5. Unless he didn't think kissing her was important. Or if he didn't think she was cute!
6. And why did he fail that exam last year? Why wouldn't he tell her about it?
7. Actually, Bee didn't really know anything about Toby. She didn't even know his surname. She didn't know how old he was, or whether he had

a girlfriend, or where he'd gone to school. All she knew was that he'd failed an exam at uni, was obsessed with cadavers and animal mating rituals and didn't like beetroot in sandwiches.

8. And he was a good kisser. That was something she knew about him.

9. STOP THINKING ABOUT KISSING HIM.

10. . . .

'Anyway, I have to go,' said Toby.

'What?' asked Bee. 'Go? Now? Where?' She tried to kickstart her brain back into full sentences, but it was still stuck on Toby's arms and lips.

'I've got a meeting with my anatomy professor.'

'You have a lot of these meetings,' said Bee, as her brain finally clicked from kissing-mode to annoyed. 'It's surprising you have time to do any work.'

'I'm sorry,' said Toby. 'I'll be in early tomorrow.'

Bee snorted. 'Sure you will,' she said. 'I hope you know there's an exhibition on in four weeks. People are counting on us, and I have to go back to school in a week.'

Toby took his glasses off and rubbed his eyes. 'I know, okay? I know. I promise I'll be here tomorrow. Just get off my back.'

'I just think you should be more conscious of your responsibilities.'

'Really?' Toby shook his head and put his glasses back on. 'You didn't seem very conscious of *your* responsibilities five minutes ago when I had my tongue in your mouth.'

Bee struggled to think up a witty comeback, while simultaneously trying not to cry with anger and experiencing a quite vivid flashback to the feeling of Toby's tongue in her mouth. But Toby wasn't waiting. He slid his phone back into his pocket and stalked out the door, slamming it behind him.

15

Bee kept her phone with her all evening. It wasn't that she thought Toby would call and apologise. It wasn't even like she cared. If he wanted to run off every time things got complicated, that was just fine with her. His loss. It wasn't as if Bee should be surprised; it seemed to be a kneejerk instinct with all men. Her father certainly hadn't stuck around, and Fletch wasn't even worth thinking about.

Bee made herself some toast for dinner, and turned on the TV. Angela and the Celestial Badger had gone out to a trivia night, some kind of fundraising event for an upcoming convention. Bee remembered Angela's giddy excitement as she'd skipped out the door, all green crushed velvet and lace, and wondered how long it would be before the Celestial Badger took up the inevitable role of masculinity and ditched her.

Bee half-watched a crime TV show that featured a dead prostitute and a highly implausible forensic investigation. She hated most crime TV shows. There was never any real detecting, the technology was ridiculous and there was never an opportunity for the viewer to solve the mystery. Once she'd finished her toast, she turned it off in disgust and checked her mobile. Nothing. Not that she was expecting anything.

She scrolled through her address book and paused at Maddy's name. She could tell Maddy all about how infuriating Toby was, and how much she didn't care if he called her or not. Maddy would be sympathetic and say all the right things and make Bee laugh. Maddy would help Bee forget about work and Toby and Featherstone and Gus. She could just press 'call', and Maddy's phone would ring. It would be easy.

Bee sighed. It was what would happen once Maddy picked up. That wouldn't be so easy. She plugged her phone into its charger and went to bed.

Bee dreamed that she was in the Red Rotunda. Adrian Featherstone was there too, bent over the glass case containing the horseshoe crab. He prised the case open, cracking the glass.

'Stop,' said Bee, but Featherstone just laughed.

He picked up the horseshoe crab, which squirmed and tried to wriggle out of his grasp. But Featherstone dug his nails into the crab's belly, pulling open its shell and ripping the crab clean in half. Glass eyes spilled out, bouncing on the floor and spinning like marbles. One of them rolled over to Bee's foot, and she bent and picked it up. It was a reptile eye. She heard a strangled cry and looked up. The black scorpion from the glass case had scrambled up Featherstone's shirt and stabbed him in the neck with its tail. Featherstone screamed, a bloodcurdling, piercing scream. Bee looked back down at the glass eye in her hand, and saw that it had turned into a real human eye, warm and glistening. She dropped it in horror, and woke up.

Ⓘ Ⓘ Ⓘ

Toby wasn't in early on Tuesday morning like he'd said he would be, but Bee wasn't surprised. She turned on the lights in the taxidermy lab, glanced at the clock on the wall (8:52), sat at her desk and pulled out the exhibition folder.

At 9:26, the door opened.

'Hi.' Toby was standing in the door of the taxidermy lab, a bunch of flowers in his hand. It was a fairly generic posy, the kind sold at the supermarket checkout for five dollars. There was a small white envelope tucked into the top.

Bee stood up, her eyes wide. 'What are you doing?' She rushed over and snatched the flowers from him. 'Are you *crazy*? Did anyone see you come in here?'

'What?'

Bee dumped the flowers into the bin by her desk, then lifted out the plastic garbage bag and tied it tightly closed. 'What on *earth* did you think you were doing?'

Without waiting for an answer, she marched out of the lab and up the stairs to the fire exit that led out to the rubbish skips. 'You can't bring flowers into the museum,' she said, over her shoulder. 'They're full of bugs that get into things and breed and eat away at all the animal fur and skin.'

There was no response from Toby and she turned. He wasn't there. Why hadn't he followed her? Bee looked at the rubbish bag in her hand and suddenly felt like an idiot. Toby had thought she'd stormed off because he'd brought her flowers. Not because he'd brought flowers *into the museum*. She swallowed and pulled the white envelope out of the bag. Inside was a card with a cartoon hedgehog holding a balloon. Bee opened the card to see small, cramped spider-writing.

HAVE I TOLD YOU ABOUT PORCUPINE COURTSHIP RITUALS? THE MALE SINGS TO THE FEMALE, AND THEN THEY REAR UP SO THEIR BELLIES TOUCH. THEN THE MALE URINATES ALL OVER THE FEMALE. ALL. OVER HER. HE COMPLETELY SOAKS HER FROM HEAD TO FOOT. SOMETIMES SHE'S NOT SEDUCED BY THIS AMAZING DISPLAY OF SEXUAL PROWESS, SO SHE YELLS AT HIM OR WHACKS HIM WITH HER FRONT PAWS. BUT IF SHE'S INTO IT, HER SPINES WILL GO ALL FLAT AND SOFT, SO THEY CAN CUDDLE WITHOUT GETTING SPIKED.

I THOUGHT IF I URINATED ALL OVER YOU, YOU MIGHT TAKE IT THE WRONG WAY, SO HERE ARE FLOWERS INSTEAD. I THINK WE'VE BEEN MISUNDERSTANDING EACH OTHER AND I WANTED TO APOLOGISE.

–TOBY

Bee dropped the rubbish bag into the skip, tucked the card into her pocket and tried not to cry. She went back downstairs, hoping that Toby would still be in the lab.

He wasn't.

One of the half-finished critters Gus had been working on was an antechinus, a tiny marsupial mousey thing with big ears and a pointed snout. It was a fiddly piece of taxidermy, and Bee had been putting off finishing it for a while. But she needed something to concentrate on, so she pulled out the prepared skin, which was no bigger than a handkerchief, and hunted around for a pair of tweezers.

She wondered what piece of bizarre antechinus trivia Toby would produce if he were there. For a moment she had a scratchy little urge to look up the antechinus on Wikipedia to learn its secrets for herself, but she frowned and forced herself to concentrate on its tiny paws. She didn't need Toby's stupid trivia in order to do her job. She'd done just fine before he'd arrived. And what with his dramatic hissyfit storm-out, it wasn't as if *he* was going to do any work, so it was up to Bee to get the exhibition ready.

She plumped up the antechinus's body with cottonwool, and inserted wire into its left leg with the tweezers, being extra careful not to puncture the skin.

Why was she even bothering to think about Toby, anyway? She should be thinking about *Featherstone.* Adrian Featherstone was a much more interesting and fruitful line of thought.

Bee was *sure* he was involved in Gus's death. He had to be. Was Toby right? Was Featherstone trying to steal Cranston's research again?

She was itching to confront Featherstone. But was it a good idea? He was clearly a corrupt man – who knew what lengths he'd go to when put under pressure? And if he *was* the murderer... Bee stared at the antechinus, who stared back unhelpfully. Bee tried to predict what might happen if she confronted Featherstone.

1. He would crumble under her razor-sharp questioning and confess his guilt.
2. He would crumble and confess *something* that would be the key to solving the mystery.
3. He would go crazy, lock Bee in his office and reveal something incriminating.
4. He would go crazy, lock Bee in his office and threaten her.
5. He would go crazy, lock Bee in his office, threaten her, *then* carry out the threats.
6. Things could go very badly for Bee.

She should wait until Toby got back. He'd probably only sulk for the rest of the day, then he'd return and say something flippant and Bee would pretend to be annoyed, and then he would win her back with his charm and everything'd be okay again. He was immature and clearly flaky, but Bee knew he'd come back. He needed his extra credit, after all. She should just wait. Featherstone wasn't going anywhere. They could talk to him tomorrow.

The antechinus seemed to think this was an excellent idea.

Bee worked solidly through the day, stopping only to grab a chicken salad sandwich from the café. Thoughts of Featherstone and Toby whirled around in her head as she methodically twisted wire, inserted cottonwool and made tiny stitches. At 5:39 PM, a grating, buzzing noise erupted from her phone. Bee jumped and nearly tore the antechinus in half.

Heart hammering, she put down the tweezers and picked up her phone. It was a text message. Bee tried very hard not to hope that it was from Toby.

> Hey sry it didnt wk out can we B frenz
> I still reckn UR cool.

That was *it*? Nearly two months after Fletch had run off with her best friend and not had the guts to break up with Bee first, and all she got was a barely decipherable text message? Saying *Sorry it didn't work out*? What about being sorry for *cheating on her with her best friend*?

Bee wondered if she was supposed to feel sad or angry. She didn't feel either emotion. In fact, she didn't feel much at all. And she never had, when it came to Fletch. She tried to remember why she'd agreed to go out with Fletch in the first place. Was it just because he'd asked and she'd been flattered by the attention? Was it because Maddy had encouraged her? *Do it, Bee. He's sooo cute. I'd totally go out with him.* That had been a warning sign she'd missed. Or had she dated Fletch because she didn't have to *think* or *feel* anything when she was with him?

Bee felt like she'd woken up from a long, featureless dream. Suddenly the world felt *real* again. Fletch hadn't challenged her or argued with her or asked her a question she didn't want to answer or bought her flowers. Not like Toby. Toby was infuriating and difficult and mysterious, but he made her feel alive.

Bee re-read the text message, trying to see if there was some subtext that she'd missed. There wasn't. There was barely text. She laughed, and wondered if it was the hysterical, upset kind of laughter that turned into tears. It didn't seem to be. The message was just funny. Stupid.

She put down her phone. Maddy was welcome to him. It was time for Bee to stop sleepwalking through life. She pushed aside thoughts of Fletch and Maddy, picked up her tweezers and turned her mind back to Adrian Featherstone.

She should wait for Toby.

Really.

It would be much more sensible to go with backup.

Bee put down the tweezers, scribbled *Gone to see Featherstone* across an index card, and propped it up against the half-finished antechinus, who looked a bit offended.

16

THERE WERE NO PREGNANT WOMEN to be seen in the Conservation offices, so Bee moved quickly and quietly towards Featherstone's office door, and tapped lightly. There was no answer.

It couldn't hurt to have another peek inside, even if he wasn't there.

Bee crept into Featherstone's office, and gently closed the door behind her. The room seemed to be in the same state of chaos as it had been the last two times Bee had visited. Or was it? Bee spotted five things that had changed.

1. An empty pizza box was balanced on top of the filing cabinet.

2. The book entitled *Secret Weapons: Defenses of Insects, Spiders, Scorpions and Other Many-Legged Creatures* was gone.

3. The badly hidden bottle of whisky was almost empty.
4. There was a street directory on the desk, open to page 449.
5. Where the nail clippings had lain on Featherstone's desk, there was now a single glass reptile eye.

Bee picked up the glass eye and examined it. It was a new one, with no scratches or marks. She remembered the missing lid on the jar in the taxidermy lab. This eye was from that jar. And it was the same as the one Featherstone had put in his pocket on the Monday after Gus had died. She was sure of it. But did that mean anything? She slipped the eye into her pocket, just in case.

'Well, hello there.'

Adrian Featherstone stood in the doorway. He smiled, stepped into the office and closed the door with a click.

Bee took an involuntary step back, and bumped into a chair.

'Sit down,' said Featherstone. 'It's so lovely to have a visitor. Why don't I make us both a nice cup of tea?'

He didn't move.

Bee sank into the chair, mostly because her knees had gone very weak. Six or seven nasty scenarios involving Adrian Featherstone flashed through her mind.

Adrian Featherstone pulled a keyring out of his pocket and shook it so the keys jangled. He selected a smallish silver key.

'So we're not disturbed,' he said, locking his office door.

He sat at his desk, closing the Melways and putting it in a drawer. Bee hoped he wouldn't notice the missing glass eye.

'So,' said Featherstone. 'You are very nosy.'

Bee noted his limp, oily hair and his unshaven jaw. He looked as though he hadn't showered in a week, and he didn't smell great either. There were dark pouches under his bloodshot eyes. Was he being haunted at night by guilty visions of his terrible crime? Was he unable to sleep because every time he closed his eyes he saw Gus's dying face?

Bee's skin crawled. Whether or not he had killed Gus – and Bee thought that the chances were high, frankly – Adrian Featherstone was still a very creepy man. *Something* was going on with him, and Bee was going to get to the bottom of it. And there was *no way* she was going to let him see that she was frightened.

Offensive. That was what she needed. To launch an offensive. Catch him off guard.

'Would you like to explain why Gus was wearing your hoodie when he died?' asked Bee. 'And why *his* hoodie is on your office floor?' She pointed.

Featherstone looked taken aback, but not as rattled as Bee had hoped.

'Been snooping around my office, have you?'

'You haven't answered my question.'

'No,' said Featherstone. 'I haven't.'

'I know who you are,' said Bee. 'I know you sold Cranston's horseshoe crab research to that pharmaceuticals company.'

She felt a surge of triumph as she saw shock flicker over Featherstone's face. 'Well,' he said. 'Aren't you clever.'

'You won't get away with this,' said Bee. She was on the front foot now. She'd spooked him. Now to sit back and see if he'd let something slip under pressure.

Featherstone seemed amused. 'Get away with what? Locking you in my office? What were you doing in here in the first place? Let's face it, it won't look good for you either.'

Bee scowled at him.

'Or do you mean I won't get away with *murdering Gus*?' He laughed. 'That's it, after all. Isn't it? You think I murdered Gus.'

'You betrayed Cranston,' said Bee. 'You cost him his chance at a Nobel Prize. You could have destroyed his entire career.'

'No,' said Adrian Featherstone, his face growing dark. 'He destroyed *my* career. I did the research. It was *me*. *My* team, not his. I've never even *met* Cranston. He sat at home in this pathetic backwater of a country, rolling around in his pots of money, paying other people to do all the hard work.'

'So you let him pay you,' said Bee. 'Then you stole the research and auctioned it off to the highest bidder.'

'You're missing the point.' Featherstone's face was mottled red and white, and his lips trembled. 'You've got this idea that Cranston is the good guy in all this. Well, he's not. There *is* no good guy. Do you know what happened afterwards? After I sold the data? Cranston *destroyed* me. He and his friends in the Royal Society smeared my name across the science world. Internationally. There wasn't a lab or a university on the planet that would hire me. He *broke* me.'

Bee took a deep breath and tried to calm herself. This was serious. Featherstone could hurt her. A lot. This wasn't Nancy Drew hijinks anymore; she'd stumbled into one of her more adult crime thrillers. She had to get out before things got ugly.

'You'll have to excuse me,' she said. 'But I'm afraid I'm struggling to dredge up any sympathy right now.'

Featherstone kicked a pile of manila folders, which slid in on themselves and then fanned out all over the floor. Bee clamped her hands firmly over her knees so Featherstone wouldn't notice how much they were trembling.

'You don't understand,' he said between clenched teeth. 'Cranston. Destroyed. My. Career. What was I supposed to do with the rest of my life?'

'I imagine the giant pile of money you got for selling him out would have presented you with some options.' Bee hoped Featherstone wouldn't hear the tremor in her voice.

'I spent it,' said Featherstone. 'Mostly on getting people to keep my name out of the press. The rest...it's amazing how fast you can spend money when you have it, and it's all there is in your life. I don't even remember what I spent it on.'

'I'm sure it was all about animal shelters and food for the homeless,' Bee said.

'Shut up,' said Featherstone, banging his hand down on his desk. 'Shut *up.*'

Bee shut up and wondered how she was going to escape. There wasn't even a window she could climb out of. Would Security have seen something? Bee didn't think there were security cameras in the staff-only areas of the museum. But surely someone would come. Eventually.

Featherstone leaned forward and rested his head on his desk. Bee waited.

'You really think I killed Gus, don't you?' he said, his voice muffled.

'I think you'd do anything to get what you want,' said Bee.

'And what is it that you think I want?'

'Revenge.' Was it really, though? Revenge was nearly always the justification for murder in detective stories – dropped like a one-word bombshell, just as she had done. But if Featherstone wanted revenge, why not just kill Cranston? Unless…

Featherstone sat up and leaned back in his chair. 'I'm terribly sorry to disappoint you,' he said. 'But I'm afraid you're wrong. Gus wasn't even working here when I arrived, and when he started I didn't realise he was really Gregory Swindon, Cranston's assistant.'

'Until you found that newspaper article,' said Bee. 'You were looking for Cranston. That's why you came to the museum in the first place.'

'I wanted to find him,' said Featherstone. 'I was hoping if I could just talk to him, explain my situation, he could help me clear my name. The ironic thing is, this museum was the one place on the planet where I could actually get a job. And it was because Cranston was a benefactor. I told Kobayashi that I'd worked for him before, and she welcomed me with open arms. Lucky for me she didn't check up on the reference letter I gave her.'

'And then Gus turned up,' said Bee. 'I find it hard to believe it was a coincidence.'

'It was the kind of luck you only dream about,' said Featherstone. 'But then, perhaps I was due a little good luck.'

Bee was torn between wanting to bang on the door and scream until someone heard, and wanting to smack Featherstone in the mouth and call him a self-pitying, spoilt child. But she did neither. She was too busy trying to sort out Featherstone's story in her head, and figure out what questions she could ask to trick him into revealing his secrets. How did Poirot do it?

'I tried to talk to Gus,' Featherstone was saying, lacing his fingers together. 'I tried to explain that I'd changed, that I was sorry—'

'You're *not* sorry,' Bee interrupted. 'I've never seen anyone less sorry.'

Adrian Featherstone glared at her. 'Beside the point,' he said. 'Gus wouldn't talk to me. He knew who I was, and he wouldn't even speak to me. Smug bastard.'

'He didn't dob you in to Kobayashi, though,' said Bee. 'He could have. He *should* have. If she'd known what you did to the museum's greatest benefactor, there's no way you would have kept your job.'

A small smile scuttled around the corners of Featherstone's mouth, making Bee wonder for a moment if she'd been too quick to dismiss Kobayashi as a suspect.

'I'm sure he was just biding his time,' said Featherstone. 'Anyway, the afternoon before he died, I saw him in the museum café. He was waiting for something – a milkshake, or a coffee. And he was sitting at a table eating a doughnut. He'd taken off his hoodie because it's so much warmer up there, with all the natural light. When he went to get whatever it was from the counter, he left his hoodie at the table for a moment. I saw my chance.'

Bee watched Featherstone through suspicious eyes. She was sure he was lying. Someone as sinister and bitter as Featherstone had to have some darker purpose than mere reconciliation. He *had* to be lying.

'I swapped our hoodies,' Featherstone was saying. 'I thought it might give me an excuse to see him. Talk to him. Explain my case. But it seems I acted too late.'

He folded his hands together and smiled insincerely.

214

'Sorry to burst your balloon,' said Featherstone. 'But you're barking up the wrong tree if you think I'm a murderer.'

Bee chose not to point out Featherstone's mixed metaphor.

'No,' said Featherstone. 'Gus and I were far from being friends, but I wouldn't have killed him.' He paused. 'And if I had, I wouldn't have been stupid enough to poison him.'

Bee swallowed.

'I mean really,' said Featherstone. 'Not *poison*. And especially not *here*. Have you ever thought, Beatrice, about all the ways you could murder someone in a museum?'

'I can't say I have,' said Bee. 'But then again, I'm not the murdering kind.'

Featherstone's lip curled. 'Think about it. I mean the obvious favourite would be the maceration tank. It's easily big enough for an adult human. I just pop you in there with plenty of water and a bucketful of liquid bacteria, shut the lid and press "go". You'll drown within a few minutes, and then the water will heat up and the bacteria will get to work. After two months there'll be nothing left but clean white bones and a lingering unpleasant smell.'

Bee's heart began to pound. Featherstone was clearly unstable. If he really had killed Gus, what would stop him from killing her as well now he knew she suspected him, and knew his history with Cranston?

'Or there's the freeze-dryer,' Featherstone continued. 'Or the flesh-eating beetles, although that might take a while and be a little conspicuous. I believe there's a few deadly spiders hanging around in the Live Exhibits studio. Or you could always just lock someone in cold storage until they froze to death.'

Bee shivered.

'Sorry,' said Featherstone. 'It's a little colder in here than the rest of the museum. A regular twenty degrees Celsius and fifty per cent humidity. We store a lot of film negatives and cellulose nitrate, and it can spontaneously combust if it gets too warm. And once it combusts, it burns with a toxic yellow smoke and is impossible to extinguish. So we like to stay cool in here. Of course, that might be a fun way to kill someone as well,' he added thoughtfully. 'A warm room and a few old film reels.'

Bee made a mental list of her options. She could:

1. Make a run for it. But Featherstone had locked the door, and she didn't want to anger him into doing something crazy – and it didn't look as if that would be hard.

2. Scream – but would anyone hear? Bee hadn't noticed any severe pregnant conservators around when she entered Featherstone's room. And screaming might also trigger the crazy-switch.
3. Somehow disable Featherstone, buying her enough time to escape.

Bee looked around the room for an object large enough to crack over Featherstone's head. A book? His computer keyboard? The chair she was sitting on? She wished she'd done the self-defence course that her mother had suggested.

Featherstone sighed. 'But I am a conservator,' he said. 'So do you know what I think I'd do?' He leaned over to his drawer and pulled out a sachet, small enough to fit snugly in the palm of his hand.

'This stuff is called Ageless,' he said. 'It's an oxygen scavenger. It sucks moisture, oxygen and corrosive gases from an object. This little sachet here will absorb up to two litres of oxygen.'

He looked at her speculatively. 'I'm guessing you weigh about fifty-five kilos,' he said. 'And your body is sixty-five per cent oxygen, which is about thirty-three litres. So if I was to put you into an airtight container along with, say, seventeen sachets of Ageless, and leave you in a cool, dark place for a few weeks…' He grinned. 'When I came back, you'd be a mummy.'

A giggle of hysterical laughter escaped Bee's lips at the word *mummy*. A nervous, uncertain look flashed across Featherstone's face, and suddenly everything fell into place. He was afraid of her. He thought she was laughing at him and that made him afraid.

Bee realised Featherstone wasn't a homicidal lunatic – he was just trying to scare her. He was trying to hide something, that was certain, but she was almost sure it wasn't Gus's murder. Featherstone wasn't a powerful, cunning killer – he was a weak, snivelling coward dressing up as an evil genius.

'Oh, come *on*,' said Bee, all fear replaced with annoyed relief. 'Don't you think that's a bridge too far?'

Featherstone seemed startled. The wavering, unsure expression returned to his eyes.

'Enough with the stupid threats,' Bee said. 'You're not going to kill me, so why don't we just cut to the chase?'

Adrian Featherstone slitted his eyes and tried to look sinister. It was almost comical. 'You think you're very clever, don't you? You think you've got me all figured out.'

'And *you* clearly think what you're doing now is intimidating. It isn't. It's just annoying. To be honest, I'm surprised you ever managed to pull off something as complicated as you did with Cranston and the horseshoe crab. You're not an arch-villain. You're just a bitter loony in desperate need of a haircut and shower.'

Featherstone snarled at her, and Bee feared she might have gone too far. Even bitter loonies could snap.

She thought she heard footsteps in the corridor outside and held her breath, hoping that whoever it was needed to see Featherstone about something. Or maybe it was the security guard come to check on her. If Faro Costa was on duty, he would have noticed. He'd have *sensed* something was wrong, with his mystical weird spiritual mojo. The footsteps slowed as they grew closer. Featherstone hadn't noticed yet; he was still spluttering and clutching the sachet of Ageless in his fist.

The knock at the door startled them both. Adrian Featherstone regained his composure and leaned across the desk. 'If you make a sound,' he said, his voice barely a whisper, 'I really will become a murderer.' He waved the sachet of Ageless in her face.

Bee rolled her eyes at him. 'Come in,' she said loudly. She heard someone try the doorhandle.

'What a pity I locked it,' said Featherstone.

The door opened. 'What a pity I have the key,' said Toby, jangling a ring of keys in his hand and stepping into the room. 'Thanks *awfully* for looking after Bee,' he said, his voice thick with sarcasm. 'Much appreciated. But we'll be heading off now.'

Featherstone didn't reply. His face betrayed no emotion at all. Bee stood up and was surprised at how trembly her legs felt. Toby held out his hand and led her from the room. Bee stopped and turned when she reached the door.

'What's hidden in the Red Rotunda?' she asked Featherstone.

He smirked condescendingly. 'Buried treasure, of course. Or perhaps a diamond necklace. It's usually diamonds in Agatha Christie, isn't it?'

He turned to a folder on his desk and began to take notes, as if nothing had happened.

BEE FOLLOWED TOBY ALONG THE back corridors of the museum, feeling relieved and grateful and a bit embarrassed. A good detective shouldn't need rescuing.

'Thanks,' she said at last.

'You're welcome.'

Bee wondered if he was still mad at her about the incident with the flowers. She'd be mad, if it were her. She felt like an idiot.

'You found my note,' she said. 'And where did you get the keys from?'

'Faro Costa,' said Toby, holding up the index card that she had left in the taxidermy lab. He didn't turn his head towards her.

'Thanks,' Bee said again.

Toby nodded.

Bee took a deep breath. 'I'm sorry I yelled at you about the flowers.'

'It wasn't supposed to be some kind of grand gesture. Just something nice.'

Bee shook her head. 'It wasn't the gesture that was the problem,' she said. 'It's just that we're not allowed to have fresh flowers in the museum. They carry all sorts of bugs that like to eat fur and skin and paper. You would have been in heaps of trouble if anyone'd caught you.'

Toby blinked. 'I didn't know.' He looked considerably cheered and Bee felt a little tingle of excitement. He had brought her *flowers*. Flowers meant something.

'No harm done,' said Bee. 'And I'm sorry I snapped.'

They reached the top of a flight of stairs, and Toby pushed open the fire door. Bee felt cool twilight air flow around her, and heard the evening rumble of the city, and crickets chirping in the bushes around the museum. It was good to be outside after being stuck in Featherstone's cramped little office.

'You know they have over four hundred distinct songs,' said Toby.

'Who?'

'Crickets. Different songs for different things, during different cycles. So there's a flirting song and a courtship song, and a mating song.'

Bee didn't say anything. She remembered Toby's hands on her body.

'You're sure you're okay?'

'Yeah,' said Bee. 'Just a bit shaken.'

Toby paused. 'So...' he said. 'I suppose I'll see you tomorrow.'

Bee bit her lip. 'Don't you want to know what I found out?' she said. 'From Featherstone?'

'Yes,' said Toby, with a rueful twist of his mouth. 'Yes, I really, really do.'

'Right then,' said Bee, grinning. 'Let's go somewhere where we can sit down. And eat. I'm *starving*.'

They wandered into the city, and ducked into a tiny Chinese restaurant where Bee ordered the biggest bowl of noodles on the menu, and three serves of dumplings. Toby raised his eyebrows and ordered a beer. Bee suddenly remembered that Toby was several years older than her and could do grown-up things like order beer.

'Well?' he said. 'Spill.'

Bee told him about Featherstone's hatred and resentment of Cranston, his wild spending, why he'd come to the museum. She told him about how Featherstone had swapped his hoodie with Gus's in an attempt to communicate with him.

'So he did it, right?' asked Toby, pinching one of Bee's dumplings. 'I mean, it's just too much of a coincidence that he *happens* to be working at the museum where Cranston's faithful employee *happens* to be killed.'

'I don't know,' said Bee through a mouthful of noodles. 'Somehow I don't think he would have told me everything he did if he was trying to conceal a murder.'

'But he's insane,' said Toby. 'I think that's been pretty clearly proven at this point. And insane people do insane things. Plus, he probably didn't think it'd matter if he told you stuff. I'm sure he doesn't see you as a threat.'

'Little does he know,' said Bee, trying to look sinister and spoiling it by having soy sauce dribble down her chin.

'Quite.'

'It all comes back to the Red Rotunda,' said Bee. 'There's something there – some secret we haven't uncovered yet.'

'You saw Cranston there the day Gus died,' said Toby, ticking things off on his fingers. 'Then Gus died in there. And Featherstone's been seen snooping around there, like he's looking for something.'

Bee pursed her lips. '*What*, though?' she asked. 'What is he looking for?'

Toby considered her, his head on one side, as though he was trying to make up his mind about something. 'What if Cranston was working on something new?' he said at last. 'Something big? What if Adrian Featherstone was trying to steal Cranston's research all over again?'

'It's possible,' said Bee. 'Likely, even. It would certainly give him a motive.'

Toby nodded. 'If he was trying to get Gus on side, and Gus wouldn't budge, it would have made Featherstone furious.'

'Furious enough to commit murder?'

'Why not?' asked Toby. 'Judging from your conversation with him, he's got a pretty black mind. I think he'd stop at nothing to get what he wanted, and if Gus was standing in the way of him getting to Cranston...'

'I suppose it would have the added bonus of revenge.'

'Exactly.'

'That's just it, though,' said Bee. 'I thought the same thing, that it was all about revenge. But now I don't know. He comes across as being this evil genius, but it's all just an act. He's greedy and nasty, but he's weak. He might have killed Cranston, but it wasn't for revenge. Murderous revenge is too... old-school for him.'

Toby laughed. 'More like Old *Testament*.'

'But in any case,' said Bee, 'it doesn't fit together. Featherstone left the building that night at eleven. And what about the fake mercuric chloride? Why would Featherstone pretend to kill Gus with a museum chemical? And how *did* he kill him, anyway?'

She slurped up the rest of her noodles, which were starting to go cold.

'I just feel like there's some trick to it all,' she said. 'Like we're looking at the whole thing from the wrong angle.'

'What do you mean?'

Bee laid her chopsticks neatly across the top of her empty noodle bowl. 'There's this guy, right?'

'If you say so.'

'And he and his dad are driving in the country one day. They're going fishing or something. And they take a bend in the road too fast and slam into a tree.'

Toby winced. 'That's no good.'

'The father is killed instantly. A passing car sees the accident and calls an ambulance. The son is seriously injured and is rushed to hospital. When he gets there, he's immediately wheeled into surgery. The doctor takes one look at him and says "Oh my God, it's my son!". How is this possible?'

'Um. Is the guy adopted? Or is his dad gay?'

Bee shook her head. 'The doctor is his *mother*.'

Toby looked a bit ashamed. 'Oops,' he said. 'Yeah. I see what you mean. Looking at it from the wrong angle.'

'It's just so easy to make assumptions.'

They walked together through Chinatown towards the train station. Silk-clad women tried to entice them into restaurants and the air was full of the smell of frying garlic. It was a muggy evening, and the air felt heavy and still, as though the city was waiting for something. Bee was tired after her long day and large meal, and she felt small and vulnerable. She wished Toby would put his arm around her shoulders. It'd be nice to have someone tall and warm to lean on, even though she was already rather damp from the humidity.

She wondered what William Cranston was doing. Was he alone on his enormous Healesville property? Was he missing Gus? She imagined Cranston and Gus sitting together in an old-fashioned kitchen, playing cards on a huge wooden table and drinking whisky. She remembered Cranston telling her that neither of them had any family. And now Cranston didn't even have Gus. How strange it must be to have someone in your life for so long, until they're like a part of you, and then one day...nothing.

'Do you believe people have souls?' she asked Toby.

Toby smiled. 'An eighteenth-century anatomist called Robert Whytt thought that the soul was split into several parts, each of which served a different function. He thought life-force was in saliva. He did an experiment where he decapitated a pigeon and then dribbled his own spit onto its heart to bring it back to life.'

'Did it work?'

'What do you think? Thomas Edison had some weird ideas about the soul, too. He said that thousands of teeny-tiny creatures live inside you and make you a person. And the reason why sometimes you can't remember stuff is because the little creatures work shifts, and maybe none of the ones who experienced a particular moment are currently on duty.'

Bee laughed. 'You haven't answered my question.'

Toby turned and looked at her. He pulled off his glasses and rubbed at his eyes, then put them back on again. 'No,' he said at last. 'I don't believe people have souls. I believe people have hearts and lungs and blood and neurons which make them function, and I believe they have brains which make them into people. Everything else is just excuses.'

'You don't believe in anything supernatural?'

'I think the world is quite full enough of mystery, horror, beauty and questions. I don't feel the need to make any more up.'

Bee nodded. 'Occam's razor,' she said.

Toby walked Bee to her platform, and they paused.

'Well,' said Toby. 'See you tomorrow?'

Bee nodded, and there was an awkward moment where she wasn't quite sure if they were supposed to hug, or even kiss. Then Toby shrugged and smiled and started to walk away. The air seemed so humid that Bee felt as if she was breathing in water. Sweat trickled down her lower back.

'Wait,' said Bee. She wasn't ready to lose the feeling of being close to Toby.

He turned around. 'Everything okay?'

'Let's go back to the museum,' she said. 'Faro Costa's on duty tonight. We could walk it through. Maybe it'll help us figure out the next step.'

Toby looked puzzled. 'Are you sure?' he said. 'You've had a pretty big day.'

'I'm sure.'

18

Faro Costa was quite happy to provide Bee and Toby with the key to the Red Rotunda.

'The sooner you find the answer,' he said, 'the sooner Gus's soul can be free and you can both come out of the shadows.'

'Thanks,' said Bee. 'Um, also?'

Faro smiled as if he already knew what she was going to say.

'I kind of have to ask you an awkward question.'

'No, I did not kill him,' said Faro. 'We have to log a report every ten minutes on the computer in the Security office. To prove we are not asleep, we have to press a button and confirm nothing strange is happening. I logged reports every ten minutes for all the time I was there. There was not time for me to go to the Red Rotunda and kill him. I can show it to you, if you like.'

'No, it's okay,' said Bee. 'Thank you. I didn't think you did kill him, but a detective has to be thorough.'

He ducked his head in a little bow. 'I will leave a print-out of the reports on your desk,' he said, and handed Toby a torch. 'Good luck.'

The museum was dark and eerie, with only the green glow of the exit signs and faint emergency lighting illuminating the major thoroughfares. The air was crisp and cool compared to the humidity outside, and Bee felt suddenly awake and alert.

Toby's torchlight glinted off the glass cases, casting looming shadows that gave the illusion of movement within them. Bee's skin crawled as she thought she saw a giant snake uncoil in the Reptile Room, and in the Great Hall she felt as if the dinosaurs could come alive at any minute and tear her to pieces.

'Creepy,' observed Toby calmly.

Bee tried to laugh.

They reached the Red Rotunda and Toby shone his torch on the door while Bee unlocked it.

'So,' he said, his voice echoing strangely in the darkness. 'Who else could have got in?'

'Well, if someone *knew* he had a copy of the key, they could have taken it from him.'

'So it could be anyone.'

'It's unlikely to be anyone who doesn't work here,' said Bee. 'But not impossible, I suppose. The next question is, how did they manage to get Gus in here?'

'You mean there's a possibility he was killed somewhere else? And his body brought here?'

'It'd be a good way to frame an employee, if that's what you wanted.'

'What if Cranston wanted to frame Featherstone?' Toby asked. 'For stealing his research? A kind of delayed justice?'

Bee thought about it. It was an interesting idea. But would he really have *murdered* his oldest friend in order to exact revenge for something Featherstone had done almost thirty years ago?

She shook her head. 'It doesn't really work. Why would Cranston make it look like Gus committed suicide if he wanted to frame Featherstone?'

Toby looked disappointed. Bee pushed open the door to the Red Rotunda, and they slipped inside.

There was no emergency lighting or exit signs in the Red Rotunda, and everything was pitch black. Toby swung the torch around a few times, and Bee shivered as she imagined the murderer – whoever it was – sneaking up behind her. Then Toby took a few steps away from her, and with one click of a light switch, blinding light filled the room. Bee screwed her eyes closed against the sudden brightness.

'Sorry,' said Toby. 'But we'll never find anything in the dark.'

Bee walked to the middle of the room, where Gus's body had been found.

'So there are only two possible solutions,' she said. 'The first is that Gus came in here, on his own, and killed himself.'

'How? The mercuric chloride was fake.'

'I don't know.'

'What's the second solution?' asked Toby.

'Someone killed him,' said Bee. 'And planted the bottle in his hand.'

'But who? And why?'

Bee wandered over to the glass cases. 'This is stupid,' she said. 'I don't know what we're doing here. We're not getting anywhere.'

She stared absently at the skeleton of a quagga. The white plaque next to it noted that it was one of only seven such skeletons in existence. She wondered what the quagga had done to deserve such an evolutionary dead end.

'So where do we go now?'

Bee shrugged. 'Home, I guess.'

'I mean, what do we do next? What's the next step?'

'I don't know.'

Toby leaned against the horseshoe crab's case. 'But you must know! WWPD?'

'Poirot would have figured it out by now,' said Bee. 'This would be the bit in *The Affair at Styles* where Poirot taps his head and says that he has to use his little grey cells to unravel the mystery. And he'd just figure it out and then annoy everyone for another four chapters by not telling them.'

'That doesn't sound like fun,' said Toby. 'What about Sherlock Holmes?'

'Holmes would be waiting for the final piece of evidence to confirm his outlandish hypothesis, but also wouldn't be telling anyone his theory, just to infuriate Watson. And Trixie Belden would realise that the answer had been staring her in the face all along.'

'Nancy Drew?'

'Nancy Drew would have some incredibly useful piece of evidence dropped in her lap. Probably along with a winning lottery ticket and a voucher for a free manicure, knowing her luck.'

'Maybe if you sat down?'

Bee looked at him.

'To make a lap,' Toby explained. 'You can't have something fall into your lap if you don't have a lap.'

Bee smiled in a distracted sort of way. She was out of ideas. She thought about all the mystery novels she'd read. She needed an *aha!* moment. One where everything would fall into place and she'd see the entire picture, clear as day. But how did she *get* that moment? There was usually a trigger. Somebody would say something innocuous and the detective would snap his or her fingers and cry *buttons! Aha!*

'Say something,' said Bee, desperately.

'What?'

'Talk about something. Tell me some useless trivia about insects.'

'Er, okay. There are about two hundred million insects for every one person. A snail can sleep for three years during a drought. Bees have five eyes – three little ones up on top and two big ones in front. Slugs have four noses. Actually, that's not true. They have a pair of gills that they breathe through, and then two things called rhinopores which help them smell.'

Bee shook her head. 'It's no good,' she said. 'I never should have started this. I'm not a detective, and life isn't an Agatha Christie novel.'

She wanted to cry, but not in front of Toby. She wanted to go home and watch TV with Angela. Or go to the movies with Maddy. Except Angela would be with the Celestial Badger. And Maddy was with Fletch. Bee was on her own.

'Come on, Bee,' said Toby. 'There must be *something* you can think of. One last idea?'

There was only one thing Bee could think of. Only one idea left.

She pulled Toby towards her and kissed him.

He stiffened in shock, but then his arms wrapped around her. He wound the fingers of one hand into her hair and cupped her head, his other arm circling her waist. She felt safe, warm, supported. It was as though she was dissolving into him, their kisses drawing them closer and closer. It drove all rational thought out of her mind, and she felt a blissful calm in the silence broken only by quick breaths.

Bee ran her hands up Toby's back, and he moaned gently, his teeth scraping Bee's lower lip in that way that made her tremble inside. He picked her up, spun her round and sat her on the glass case.

He kissed her cheek, her lips, her throat. He started to pull up her T-shirt, but then drew away, panting a little.

'I didn't think you wanted to do this,' he said. 'You didn't say anything, after last time.'

Bee raised an eyebrow. 'Neither did you.'

'I didn't think you wanted me to.'

'Why?'

'Because you didn't say anything.'

Bee looked down at the horseshoe crab. Next to it, the deathstalker scorpion glared up at her, its tail poised, ready to strike.

'I thought we had fun,' said Toby. 'On the tiger.'

'We did.' Bee felt a sudden rush of warmth at the memory. Why was Toby talking? What had happened to the kissing? Bee had liked the kissing.

'So...'

'So what?'

'So why didn't you say anything?'

Bee looked up from the case. Why did they have to talk about this? 'Because our boss was murdered and I had other things on my mind. Also, you didn't show any indication that you actually liked me.'

'I *kissed* you. Three times. Although technically this last time you kissed me.'

'I've kissed plenty of people I don't like.' This wasn't strictly true. Bee had only kissed Fletch before Toby, and she hadn't disliked him, she'd just found him dull. But how *dare* Toby accuse her of not making her feelings clear? What was she supposed to do, wear a sign around her neck? Get a skywriter?

Toby's cheeks were flushed, and somewhere at the back of Bee's mind she registered that she had genuinely hurt him. But the angry bit at the front of her mind was louder.

'Every time you kiss me,' she said, 'you leave immediately afterwards. We don't ever talk about anything, because you're too busy answering your mysterious phone calls. You don't know anything about me.'

'Well, *sorry*,' said Toby, his face clamming up. 'I didn't realise we were having a *relationship*.'

What? He stopped the kissing to talk about their feelings, and now he was trying to play the aloof male card? Did he like her or not?

'Who said anything about a relationship?' What was *wrong* with him?

'You did. Just then.'

'No I didn't! I never said I wanted to have a relationship with you,' said Bee, trying to decide whether to try to kiss him again, or punch him in the face. 'Right now I'm not sure I want to be having a *conversation* with you.'

'But you said—'

Bee gritted her teeth. 'I don't want to have a relationship with you. But if we're going to be making out up against display cases or on stuffed tigers, I want it to be because you want to make out up against a display case

238

or on a stuffed tiger *with me*. Not just because you want to be making out, and I happen to be there.'

'So you don't want me to make out with anyone else?'

'That wasn't at all what I was saying, but, no, now that you mention it, I don't want you to make out with anyone else.'

'Because that's my definition of a relationship.'

Bee laughed, a little hysterically. 'Your definition of a relationship is not kissing anyone else?'

'Sure.'

She shook her head. 'I'm beginning to understand why it is you haven't been snapped up yet.'

'How do you know I haven't? There are plenty of girls who would *love* to snap me up.'

'This is ridiculous.' Bee suddenly felt the eyes of cats, dogs, spiders, toads, a horseshoe crab and a very fierce scorpion staring at her.

'*You're* ridiculous,' he said. 'You have no idea what you want, do you? You're just running around pretending to be Beatrice Ross, Girl Detective, and ignoring the fact that the world is going on all around you.'

A small part of Bee was surprised that Toby even knew her surname, but it was overtaken by a much bigger part that was marauding angrily through her.

'Well, at least I'm not the one who's stuck here all summer because I *failed my exams*,' she said. 'You want to talk about ignoring the world going by? Why'd you fail, Toby? Too busy with your social life? I can just imagine you out every night, getting drunk and picking up any girl who'd listen to your stupid animal trivia. I bet you've had girls pressed up against display cases in every museum and library in the state.'

Toby opened his mouth to retort, then shut it again with a snap. 'You don't know anything about me either,' he said finally, his voice low and angry. 'You don't know what happened to me last year. You don't know about my life. And you don't even want to find out. You'd rather add up all your little clues and observances and fabricate stories about people so they fit your perfect storybook idea of how the world works. Where every mystery has a villain and every death can be solved if you follow a trail of breadcrumbs. Well, let me tell you, I'm not the villain of your story. I don't even want to be *in* it.'

Bee couldn't reply. Toby was right. Everything he had said was right. She *had* been running around ignoring the real world. She'd been ignoring the fact that her mother had a new boyfriend and was starting a whole new part of her life, a new part that didn't include Bee. What if Angela wanted the Celestial Badger to move in with

240

them? What if they got married? What if Angela got pregnant and Bee suddenly had a baby Badger brother or sister? And Bee was ignoring the fact she'd lost her boyfriend and her best friend. What was going to happen when school started? Would Fletch and Maddy be walking around together? Holding hands? Kissing in public? Who would Bee sit with at lunchtime? Would everyone think she was a loser because she'd been abandoned by her friend *and* her boyfriend?

Life wasn't a detective novel. You couldn't just be objective and stand back and believe everything would work itself out. Life was messy and had a way of tangling you up in its messiness and making everything all knotted and confusing. Not every crime had a villain. Not every question had an answer. Not every mystery had a neat solution.

Toby was watching her as though he was waiting for her to say something. Bee realised she was still sitting on the glass case. She slid off it and straightened her T-shirt, feeling awkward and embarrassed. She didn't say anything.

Toby shook his head and turned to walk away. 'Forget it,' he said. 'I'm done being your sidekick.'

19

Toby didn't come to work on Wednesday. Or Thursday.

On Friday morning, Bee picked up the salt-crusted koala skin that Toby had been working on, dusted it off and set about making its wireframe skeleton.

She mechanically wound cottonwool around wire and referred to the anatomical diagrams in *Anatomy of Australian Mammals*, trying not to think. There was no safe avenue of thought. She didn't want to think about Toby, or Gus, or Featherstone, or Fletch and Maddy, or Angela and the Celestial Badger. Every single one of them made her insides squirm with anxiety or disappointment.

Instead, Bee occupied herself by listing the titles and key features of Nancy Drew books in chronological order, starting in 1930 with *The Secret of the Old Clock*. She became briefly stuck in 1940, but then remembered *The Mystery of the Brass-Bound Trunk* and continued. The koala didn't help, but it also didn't interrupt her flow of thought as she packed its paws full of wire and cottonwool. At 1954 (*The Scarlet Slipper Mystery*), Bee paused to stretch and adjust the height of her chair.

She worked and worked in a kind of trance, where murderers and good kissers and ex-best friends and Badgers didn't exist. Just her, a dead koala, a bag of cottonwool and several hundred Nancy Drew titles. She stopped briefly at 2:27 PM (1974, *The Mystery of the Glowing Eye*) to grab a sandwich from the café, then sank back into the trance.

The general hum of the museum quietened at 6:15 PM (1989, *The Girl Who Couldn't Remember*), as the visitors and most of the staff left.

At 8:33 PM (1995, *The Riddle in the Rare Book*), Bee's stomach rumbled, but she was nearly finished the koala, so she ignored it.

When the white phone on the wall rang at 9:43 PM (2002, *Mystery by Moonlight*), Bee started so violently she almost stabbed herself in the face with a pair of pliers. Heart hammering and eyes wide from being jolted out of her trance, she answered the phone with a shaky hand.

It was Akiko Kobayashi.

'It's Bee, isn't it?' she said. 'Do you think you could meet me in the Conservation lab? There's something I need to discuss with you. About Gus.'

Bee's mind snapped into focus. Did Kobayashi have some new information? She must have found out from Faro Costa or someone else that Bee was investigating Gus's death.

Bee drank a glass of water to drive away the dizzy, hungry feeling, before hurrying out the door of the taxidermy lab.

The Conservation studio was as blindingly lit and spotless as always, and totally empty, except for the low hum and occasional blinking light of various kinds of technical equipment that Gus would have turned his nose up at.

Bee perched on a stool to wait for Kobayashi. There was a plastic container full of glass reptile eyes sitting on a bench. Bee stared at them, and they glinted back at her, the vertical slits of the pupils alien and malevolent. Bee tried to think of nice eyes. Deer. Deer had nice eyes. And alpacas. She thought about how William Cranston's eyes were the palest of pale blues, so he always looked startled. What colour had Gus's eyes been? She couldn't remember. She remembered his shaggy eyebrows and the dark pouches under his eyes, but not the colour.

She thought she heard something from the corner of the room where a white curtain was hung in front of a complicated camera, ready to photograph objects. Bee held her breath, but didn't hear anything else. It must have just been the building creaking. Or maybe a mouse.

She dug in her pocket and pulled out the article about Cranston and Gus that she had been carrying around all week. She looked at the two men. There was William Cranston on the right, holding the shotgun. He smiled out at Bee, his pale eyes startling even in black and white. Gus's downcast eyes, in contrast, looked almost black. Bee wondered what he was looking at. Something towards the lower right-hand corner of the photo. She re-read the caption.

Scientist and Museum Benefactor William Cranston with his assistant, Gregory Uriel Swindon.

A thought twitched at the back of her mind as she heard the clipping of high heels from the corridor outside.

'Beatrice May Ross,' said Akiko Kobayashi from the doorway. 'Girl Detective.'

Bee felt suddenly unsteady on her stool. Something wasn't right.

'I think it's time we had a little chat,' said Kobayashi.

Kobayashi was smiling, but not in a warm and fuzzy kind of way. Her heels clicked on the floor as she walked towards Bee.

'You need to stop whatever game you think you're playing.'

Bee frowned. 'Why?'

'I told you the other day. The museum is having money trouble. We're trying to attract new philanthropic support. The new exhibition *must* go smoothly, and the last thing I need right now is unwanted media attention about some crazy murder story you've invented.'

'It's not invented,' said Bee. 'Gus wasn't his real name. He was Gregory Uriel Swindon, and he used to work for William Cranston. And he was murdered.'

Kobayashi sighed. 'Gus killed himself. It's unfortunate, but he was a lonely old man, and these things happen. That's it. End of story. Nobody was murdered. You have no suspects. You have no case. You have no evidence. Stop playing detective and do your job.'

Bee felt uneasy. Was she in trouble again? Toby wouldn't come and rescue her this time. Not that Bee wanted him to. She took a deep breath. She wasn't going to let herself be intimidated.

'How much do you know about Adrian Featherstone?' she asked. 'Did you know he used to work for a company called BioFresh? Did you know he stole research from William Cranston, and sold it to a pharmaceuticals company for millions of dollars? Did you know that on the day before Gus died, Featherstone swapped his hoodie with Gus's? So that he could get to Gus?'

Kobayashi didn't bat an eyelid. 'Adrian Featherstone is a valued member of our staff. He has done nothing but devote himself to the welfare of this institution.'

She knew. Kobayashi knew about Gus's real identity, and she knew about Featherstone, Bee was sure of it. What was going on?

'What were the eyes for?' asked Bee, suddenly.

'The what?'

'The reptile eyes,' Bee repeated. 'The ones in the pocket of the hoodie that Gus was wearing when he died. Featherstone's hoodie.'

'I don't know what you're talking about,' said Kobayashi. 'But I suppose if you're very curious you could ask Adrian yourself.'

She turned towards the curtained-off photography area. Bee went cold, and as every hope in her body sank into dread, she heard the squeak of rubber-soled shoes on linoleum. Adrian Featherstone walked out from behind the curtain, carrying a clipboard, as if he'd just been doing a little late-night work.

'Hello, Beatrice,' he said.

Bee swallowed, but raised her chin. 'What were the eyes for?' she asked again.

Adrian Featherstone chuckled. 'Really?' he said. 'Are we still doing this? You still think I'm a murderer?'

He glanced in the direction of Kobayashi, who looked uncomfortable.

'Just tell me,' Bee snapped. 'Without all the theatrics.'

Featherstone looked a bit disappointed. 'Some of the specimens we got in from that museum in Canberra had glass eyes that were treated with a lead-based paint,' he said. 'I removed them and selected some replacements from the taxidermy lab.'

'Were the eyes in the pocket the old ones? Or the new ones?'

'Why does it matter?'

'The old ones or the new ones?'

'The old ones. I needed them to compare the sizes.'

Bee narrowed her eyes. 'So you had lead-coated eyes in the pocket of the hoodie that you then planted on Gus?' She looked at Kobayashi. 'Would that have been enough to kill him?' she asked. 'The lead?'

Featherstone laughed again. 'Nice try. But even if Gus had *eaten* the eyes they wouldn't have killed him. Not for a few years, anyway.'

Bee stared at both of them and realised something. 'You're working together.'

Kobayashi looked down at the floor. 'Of course we work together,' she said, swallowing. 'I'm his boss.'

'He's offered you money, hasn't he?' asked Bee. 'When he steals Cranston's research again and sells it to the highest bidder, you think the money will be enough to get the museum out of its debt.'

'I don't know what you're talking about.'

'But what does he get in return?' wondered Bee aloud. 'Are you giving him information on Cranston? Where he lives? You must have details, because Cranston's donated money to the museum before. You're helping him get to Cranston. Right?'

Kobayashi said nothing.

'Or did you catch him?' asked Bee. 'Did you find out what he was doing, and threaten to turn him over to the police? And he's bought your silence?'

The corner of Kobayashi's eyelid twitched.

'This is all very entertaining,' said Adrian Featherstone, looking bored.

Bee ignored him. 'Did you do it?' she asked Kobayashi. 'Did you kill Gus?'

Kobayashi's eyes flicked to Adrian Featherstone. 'What you're suggesting is completely untrue,' she said. 'But even if it were true, I am no murderer. And neither is Adrian. So you just need to get your pesky little nose out of what are *confidential business matters* concerning the museum. Not you.'

'So where were you when Gus died?'

Kobayashi seemed to regain a little of her confidence. 'Are you asking for my *alibi*?' she said. 'You really are taking this whole thing very seriously, aren't you?'

'You didn't answer my question.'

'Fine,' said Kobayashi. 'I was at home. In bed. Asleep.'

'Any witnesses who can verify that?'

Kobayashi rolled her eyes. 'My *husband*.'

Bee found she couldn't quite imagine Kobayashi with a husband. She hoped he had the good sense to do everything she told him.

'So what's *your* alibi?' asked Kobayashi.

Bee frowned. She didn't need an alibi. She was the *detective*. Then she remembered an Agatha Christie novel where the narrator turned out to be the murderer. It was a fair enough question. 'Toby can attest to my whereabouts,' she said. 'We were together the whole night.'

'Were you?' asked Kobayashi, with flinty eyes. 'Are you sure about that? You were together the *whole time*?'

What was she talking about? Then Bee remembered. After they'd heard a noise and climbed off the tiger, Toby had vanished. Looking for the security guard, he'd said. And he'd claimed that he couldn't find anyone. But Faro Costa had told them he'd been in the control room at the time. So where *had* Toby gone? And *how did Kobayashi know about it?*

Bee caught her breath. She remembered Toby's evasiveness about why he'd failed his exams. She thought about the strange phone calls and his mysterious meetings with his anatomy lecturer. How *had* he been able to find out so much about Cranston and Adrian Featherstone? Was it really all information you could look up on a database?

Bee swallowed as she remembered the weird vibe between Kobayashi and Toby, when they had gone to question her about Gus the first time. What if she'd been on the right track with her suspicion that Kobayashi and Featherstone were having an affair, except that instead of Featherstone, Kobayashi was sleeping with *Toby*? Bee felt a bit sick.

'But what if you're in it together?' asked Kobayashi. 'In fact, you and Toby are the only people who Security can verify as being in the building at the time of Gus's death. I'm pretty sure that wouldn't look good. If I happened to go to the police.'

Bee shivered. 'I didn't murder Gus, and you know it.'

'I do know it,' said Kobayashi, 'because Gus killed himself. So you need to stop running around this workplace accusing my employees of murder.'

Bee said nothing.

'So if I were you,' Kobayashi said with a businesslike nod, 'I would finish up my work in the lab, and then go back to doing whatever it is that teenagers do.'

'Drugs,' said Featherstone.

'Or school,' said Kobayashi. 'Whichever you prefer.'

'You're blackmailing me,' said Bee.

Kobayashi smiled. 'Let me assure you, there is no blackmail in the museum. I'm just trying to maintain a harmonious working environment for my staff.'

'Fine,' said Bee. 'Fine, I'll go. Is that okay? Can I go? You don't want to lock me in a freezer or stuff me into an airtight container or something first?' She shot a dark look at Featherstone.

'Don't be ridiculous,' said Kobayashi. 'Now, it's late. I'm sure your parents are worried about you.'

Bee slid off her stool and walked to the door of the Conservation studio. Kobayashi and Featherstone didn't move as they watched her go. Bee felt like a small furry animal, trapped between two birds of prey.

'Goodnight, Bee,' said Kobayashi. 'Have a lovely week-end. I suppose I'll see you at the funeral.'

☽ ☽ ☽

Bee arrived home to find Angela's bedroom door closed and low voices coming from inside. Bee made a face as she imagined what might be going on in there. She went into her room without turning on the light, and sat on her bed in darkness, thinking.

Kobayashi was right. She and Toby were the only people who had been seen in the museum that night. *They* were the key suspects.

Bee padded over to her laptop, switched it on and opened a web browser, squinting in the sudden light.

She navigated to the University of Melbourne home page, and tried to find the anatomy department. Nothing. She tried typing 'anatomy' into the staff search box, but also came up with nothing. A similar search for subjects also returned no results. Finally, she typed 'anatomy' and 'University of Melbourne' into Google, and found a long page about the Faculty of Biomedicine. Buried in long paragraphs of text about key course deliverables and assessment criteria, there was a line that read *the fundamentals of human anatomy are incorporated into various aspects of the undergraduate degree.*

So who was this professor of anatomy that Toby had been getting all his information from?

A list of possible explanations popped into Bee's head, each more ridiculous than the first. Was Toby a government spy? Was he secretly working for Cranston? Or Kobayashi? Had he been promised a cut of the money too?

Bee thought about his hands on her, the way his kisses made her feel dizzy and hot and alive. She thought about his nerdy insect trivia and his cheeky grin. Then she pushed it all out of her mind. A detective had to be impartial. Clinical. Detached.

There was really only one explanation that made sense.

Toby was working for Featherstone. He'd been in on it all along. That's how he'd found out about everything so easily.

Could it be a coincidence that Toby had started work at the museum on the same day Gus died?

He'd left her for sixteen minutes after the incident in the Catacombs. He'd got her drunk and then confused her with kissing and tigers. Then he'd disappeared.

Had Toby murdered Gus?

20

BEE SLIPPED IN AND OUT of sleep, her dreams uneasy and full of stuffed possums and horseshoe crabs and the deathstalker scorpion. As soon as her alarm clock clicked over to nine o'clock on Saturday morning, she picked up her phone.

She toyed with it for a moment, then tapped out a message to Toby.

Cafe. Now. Urgent.

There was a possibility he wouldn't come. There was a possibility that he was a murderer and Bee was going to meet a sticky end. There was a possibility she'd got it all wrong and they'd laugh it off and then hold hands and make goofy eyes at each other. But either way, she had to know.

255

Toby was already there when she arrived, looking rumpled, as if she'd woken him up, which she almost certainly had. The sight of his sleepy eyes behind slightly askew glasses made Bee's heart leap, and she sternly squashed it. She had to put aside her feelings for Toby – and she did have feelings, she was brave enough to admit that. But the truth was more important.

The expression on his face when Bee slid into the chair opposite him nearly broke her heart.

'I was hoping you'd call,' he said, with a fluttery little smile. 'I've got a lot I want to tell you.'

Bee swallowed and told herself it was all an act. Toby was trying to trick her into believing him. She'd *seen* him turn the charm on, to Kobayashi, to the severe pregnant conservators. And here he was doing it to her. She mustn't fall for it.

'I want to apologise,' he said. 'I don't think—'

'No,' said Bee. 'Wait. I need to ask—'

Toby put up his hands. 'Let me go first,' he said. 'Please,' he added, with a look that nearly made Bee crumble. She nodded as she struggled to regain her steely resolve.

'Right,' said Toby. 'So, the first thing is...' He trailed off and looked flustered, running a hand through his hair. 'Penguins,' he said. 'I want to tell you about penguins.

Penguins mate for life, and when a male Adélie penguin has found the lady penguin of his dreams, he tells her by rolling a stone at her feet. It's like this special gift, because most of the stones are used to build walls around nests and there aren't many spare ones. In fact, sometimes the male penguins pinch each other's stones. Anyway. If the lady penguin accepts the gift of the stone, the two penguins stand opposite each other, with their bellies pressed together, and sing a mating song, heads thrown back, their flippers spread wide and trembling. So, what I want to say is that you should take this speech as a metaphorical stone-rolling. Because I'm sorry. I'm sorry for being a dickhead and I'm sorry I said everything wrong and I'm sorry if I didn't make my feelings clear. I like you. I like spending time with you. I think you're funny and smart and pretty and although you're *really* bossy and you think you're always right, well, most of the time you are. And I would like to spend more time with you, having conversations and holding hands and doing all of that stuff that people who like each other are supposed to do. As well as the stuff on display cases and tigers, because I want to do that too.'

Bee felt as if she was going to burst into tears. But she swallowed and had a few stern words with herself.

'Stop,' she said. That seemed like a good start.

Toby looked a bit taken aback, as though he'd expected his penguin speech to have a different effect. It gave Bee the strength to go on.

'I need to ask you a few questions,' she said. 'About the night Gus was murdered.'

Toby blinked. 'Go on.'

'When you said you were going to Security,' said Bee. 'After we were in the Catacombs. Where did you go?'

Toby broke eye contact with her for the first time since she'd sat down. Bee's heart sank. So it was true.

'What do you mean?' he said. 'I went to Security.'

Bee shook her head. 'No, you didn't. Faro Costa said he was there that whole time. You said you didn't see anyone. Where did you go?'

Toby said nothing. A tear slid down Bee's cheek.

'You did it, didn't you?' she asked. 'You killed Gus.'

He didn't deny it. He just sat there, his face frozen, his eyes locked on his hands, which were folded on the laminex table.

'Oh my God,' whispered Bee.

How could she have been so blind? It had been Toby all along. And here he was, practically admitting it.

Finally he raised his head and looked at her. His eyes were so full of hurt and sadness that Bee thought she might break apart.

'Is that... really what you think?' he said, his voice very low. 'You think I killed Gus?'

Bee bit her lip.

Toby's face darkened. 'Well, then,' he said. 'It seems that...' He shook his head. 'I think you underestimated me. And I think I overestimated you.'

He put his hands up and rubbed his temples. 'Fine. You want the truth?' He nodded, as if having an internal conversation with himself. 'The truth, then.'

Bee felt herself tense.

Toby leaned forward. 'I'm not a second-year med student. I'm actually doing a PhD.' He saw Bee's reaction and gave an ironic grin. 'Don't worry, I didn't lie about my age. I'm nineteen. I'm... really good at science. I did university-level biology when I was in high school, and when I graduated I got fast-tracked into a PhD. I'm studying the phylogenetic significance of microsatellites in monotreme chromosomes. Anyway. The Dean of Zoology at my uni is my supervisor. I've known him since I started going to the university when I was thirteen, so we're pretty good mates. He's quite a famous scientist, and he's a Fellow of the Royal Society in the UK.'

Toby was talking fast, looking at his hands. Bee wondered if she could trust him. She really, really wanted to. But was she just letting her feelings get in the way? It was a classic detective's mistake. Get involved, lose your objectivity. It never ended well.

'So the Dean asked me for a favour. The Royal Society were conducting an investigation into a renegade scientist called Adrian Featherstone, who had stolen some important research twenty-five years ago and sold it to a pharmaceuticals company. There'd been reports that he'd recently made contact with some shady organisation that pays big money to sell on research to the pharmaceuticals industry, and the Royal Society wanted to know more, without spooking him. The scientist happened to now be working at the museum. I was young, unknown and inconspicuous. The Dean knew he could trust me. So he asked if I could go to the museum posing as a volunteer needing extra credit, and see if I could find anything out.'

'So you're...a spy?' Bee's hormones were waging an out-and-out battle with the rational part of her brain. She didn't know what to think.

Toby shrugged. 'Sort of,' he said. 'Without the disguise or the concealed weapon. That night, the night Gus died? I didn't go to Security, you're right. I went to Featherstone's office. I thought it might be a good opportunity to do some snooping. But I ran into Kobayashi in the corridor and had to turn back.'

Bee couldn't think of anything to say.

Toby sighed. 'I don't really care if you believe me or not. You don't ever have to see me again.'

Bee felt as if someone had punched her in the stomach. 'Why?'

Toby took off his glasses and rubbed his eyes. 'Because I'm done. My investigation is over. That was the other thing I was going to tell you. And you can choose not to believe me, but I'll tell you anyway and then I'll get out of your life and you can decide whether I'm a murderer or not. I'll even leave you my address in case you need to send the cops over.'

Bee felt like the very filthiest kind of rat. The objective side of her was starting to agree with the hormonal side. Toby wasn't a murderer. The relief that started to seep through Bee was drowned out by a wave of misery. Toby looked so hurt and betrayed. And he'd just said that he never wanted to see her again.

'The Dean called me last night,' said Toby. 'He said that Cranston had submitted a paper to the Royal Society and the Nobel Committee. It was the results from all his latest work. Cranston has been doing this top-secret research using scorpion venom. It contains a bunch of neurotoxins that are not usually life-threatening to a normal healthy adult, but can send a child or an old or sick person into anaphylactic shock. But there's one element of the venom, called a chlorotoxin, that Cranston's been concentrating on particularly. Because his research has shown that this chlorotoxin attacks cancerous cells in the brain before it attacks healthy ones. Cranston's been working on a possible cure for cancer.'

'Oh,' whispered Bee.

'So that's it,' said Toby. 'I'm done. If Featherstone was planning on stealing Cranston's work, he's too late.'

He stood up and threw a five-dollar note onto the table next to his empty coffee cup. Then he left without saying another word.

Bee stared down at the laminex table. Everything was wrong. Toby wasn't the murderer – but she'd ruined everything with him. Any chance of a possible romance or friendship.

And to make matters worse, Bee had about forty-seven hours left before she had to go back to school, and she was no closer to solving the mystery of Gus's death.

☾ ☾ ☾

The Celestial Badger was coming out Bee's front door when Bee arrived home at quarter past eleven.

'You were up early,' he said, then looked at her properly. 'Are you okay?'

'I'm fine,' said Bee. She wasn't fine, but the last person she wanted to talk to about it was her mother's boyfriend. Okay, maybe not the last. She couldn't really bear the thought of talking to Toby, either. Or Featherstone or Kobayashi. The Celestial Badger was maybe the fourth-last person she wanted to talk to about it.

What she really wanted was to talk to Maddy. Maddy wouldn't be able to solve any of Bee's problems, but she'd listen and ask the right questions and then say something funny to make Bee see that perhaps things weren't that bad after all. But Bee couldn't talk to Maddy, because Maddy was with Fletch. And Fletch was a cheating idiot, which made Maddy the kind of girl who would ditch her best friend for a cheating idiot. Not exactly the kind of person you wanted to take advice from.

'You don't look fine.'

Bee was surprised to find herself still standing on her own porch, the Celestial Badger hovering around and looking worried.

'I'm just tired,' said Bee, then burst into tears.

The Celestial Badger flushed red with embarrassment, then tremblingly put an arm around Bee, making sure none of his torso touched hers. 'There, there,' he said, patting her shoulder awkwardly. 'Do you want to talk about it?'

His tone of voice suggested that he vehemently hoped she didn't.

'No,' said Bee. The Badger looked relieved.

Then Bee started talking, almost against her will. And not about Cranston and Gus and Featherstone, or even about Toby. She started talking about Maddy and the whole mess with Fletch.

'I just really miss her,' she said. 'I wish there was some way we could be friends again.'

'Isn't there?'

Bee looked at the Celestial Badger and tried to see what her mother found attractive. 'I don't think so.'

'But you *want* to be friends again. And so does she.'

'But she's dating my ex-boyfriend. Which she started doing *before* he was my ex-boyfriend.'

'So?'

Bee shook her head. 'You don't understand.'

'No, I don't. If you both want to be friends, and you're not angry at her anymore, then who cares who she's dating? Isn't friendship supposed to be more important than boys?'

Bee didn't say anything. Was it possible that the Celestial Badger was right? Could it be that simple? She stood up.

'Thanks for listening,' she said. 'And...thanks for looking after my mum.'

'It's my pleasure,' he said with a somewhat goofy smile. 'Enjoy your Saturday, and make sure you get a good night's sleep. You'll feel much better tomorrow. Like a whole new person.'

21

Bee's alarm went off at seven-thirty on Sunday morning, but she thumped it and went back to sleep.

She woke again at 8:59, and stretched out in bed. Gus's funeral was at eleven, but she wasn't going. And she wasn't going back to the museum, either. Ever again. She'd been threatened by Kobayashi and Featherstone and it wasn't as though Toby would be there to back her up. Screw them all. They could have their murderer. It wasn't her problem. She'd tried to help, but everyone seemed equally corrupt and unpleasant. And it was too big, anyway. Too big a mystery for Bee. It wasn't just missing jewels or a long-lost sibling. This was murder and blackmail and stealing important scientific research.

At 9:26 AM, Bee emerged from her bedroom. Her mother was sitting on the couch, scowling at some mail.

'Everything okay?' asked Bee, wandering into the kitchen for coffee.

'Just bills,' said Angela. 'I'm going to have to take on another class. Being a grown-up sucks.'

Bee made a face. 'Try being a teenager.'

'Been there, done that. Fewer bills.'

Bee peered into the coffee plunger and shrugged. Lukewarm was better than nothing.

'Other things that suck about being an adult include taxes, parking fines, remembering when to put the bins out and having to earn an honest living but not be able to spend my hard-won earnings on the new Final Fantasy game, because the water bill is due.'

Bee pulled a *Lord of the Rings* movie tie-in mug from the cupboard, and poured herself a coffee.

'You've been out a lot lately,' said Angela.

'Work has been busy.'

'But you're finished now, right? And back to school tomorrow?'

School. What a crazy thought.

'I'm worried you haven't had a proper holiday,' said Angela. 'You're supposed to be resting up. This year will be a big one.'

Bee sipped the warmish coffee and screwed up her nose. 'I'll be fine,' she said. There was no way Year Twelve was going to be as intense as her summer break. It'd be a breeze.

Angela put down her bills and hesitated. 'Did you...see Neal yesterday? You came in just after he left. I thought I heard you talking.'

Bee nodded. 'We passed each other on the doorstep and had a chat.'

'What about?'

'Stuff. I was tired and grumpy. He gave me some good advice.'

'What kind of advice?' Angela toyed with the amethyst ring on her finger.

Bee frowned. What *was* it that the Celestial Badger had said to her? He said she should be friends with Maddy again. She remembered that part. But there was something else...

'Do you like him?'

'What?' said Bee. 'Oh. Sure, he seems really nice.'

Something about sleep. He'd told her to go to sleep...

'I just want you to be okay with all this,' said Angela. 'I know I totally failed to provide you with a decent father the first time around. And I know how upset you were when he left, although you probably don't remember much now. You were so little.'

Get a good night's sleep. He'd said that. Then what?

268

'I know sometimes I'm a bit of a flaky mum,' Angela continued. 'And I'm certainly not like other mothers. I know you used to be embarrassed by me when you were younger, and I'm sorry if I've ever made you uncomfortable by being a giant nerd.'

The image of a jar of glass eyes kept popping into Bee's mind. But they weren't reptile eyes. They were blue. Pale, startled blue, like William Cranston's eyes, smiling and sparkling at the camera.

'Anyway,' Angela said, 'I suppose I just wanted to hear that you're okay with me seeing Neal. And I wanted to reassure you that you're still my biggest priority, even though there's this new person in my life. You're still number one.'

Bee's head snapped up. 'New person,' she repeated.

Make sure you get a good night's sleep. You'll feel much better tomorrow. Like a whole new person.

Bee dropped her coffee mug, which shattered on the kitchen floor, splashing her feet with tepid coffee.

'Bee?' Angela hurried into the kitchen. 'Are you okay?'

Bee didn't respond. Angela bent down and started picking up shards of mug. 'Don't move,' she said. 'You've got bare feet.'

'A whole new person,' said Bee.

'What?' Angela picked up a fragment of mug and looked at it. 'Poor Aragorn.'

Bee gazed at the pool of coffee on the floor, her mind whirling. She was on the edge of something. Something big. She felt as if she had almost all the pieces of the puzzle, but she just wasn't sure how to go about putting them together. She suddenly remembered seeing a news report the night Gus had died. Something about an attempted burglary...

'Street directory,' she said out loud. 'Do we have a street directory?'

Angela blinked. 'On the bookshelf,' she said.

Bee picked her way over broken bits of mug to the living room, tugged the street directory off the bookshelf and thumbed through it until she found page 449. She stared at it, her mind full of suspects and alibis and the words *like a whole new person*.

'I need to talk to Toby,' she said. She up-ended her handbag onto the couch, spilling lip gloss, sunglasses, a dollar-seventy in loose change and a rogue tampon. She fished her phone out of the debris and brought up Toby's number, her hands shaking. The phone rang, and rang, and rang, before finally clicking over to voicemail.

No surprise, really. If Toby had accused Bee of murder, she probably wouldn't want to talk to him either.

'Fine, then,' she said. 'I'll go to Gus's funeral.'

'Good,' said Angela. 'I think maybe you need some closure on this.'

Bee scooped everything back into her bag, and headed for the front door.

'Um,' said Angela. 'Bee? I know I'm hardly one to judge people for their sartorial self-expression, but are you sure your Rupert Bear pyjamas are the best choice of outfit for a funeral?'

ⓘ ⓘ ⓘ

In movies, funerals always took place on dreary, grey days where rain slid down car windows and off umbrellas like oily tears.

Bee pulled at her collar and wished life was more like the movies. The sun was blazing hot – the kind of heat that felt as if someone was pummelling her head in with a lead hammer. As soon as Bee had stepped off the train, she'd regretted wearing stockings. Her feet felt as though they had swollen to double their usual size in her tight black shoes, and the back of her shirt was damp and sticky with sweat.

There were only six people at the gravesite: Kobayashi in an immaculate, elegantly structural black dress, very high heels and large sunglasses; Bee; two of the guys from the Moulding and Casting studio at the museum; a civil celebrant; and, lurking a little way away from the others, Toby. Bee's heartbeat quickened when she saw him, and she felt her knees tremble. She tried to catch his eye, but he wouldn't look at her.

The heat was relentless, and there was no shade. Bee wished she'd brought a bottle of water. Or a hat.

The celebrant seemed to be waiting for more mourners to arrive, but after ten minutes she gave up and took her place at the head of the grave. Bee felt a little dizzy, and wondered if she was getting sunstroke.

The celebrant said a few generic, meaningless things and surreptitiously tried to swat a fly that was buzzing around her head.

Bee noticed a black, expensive car pull up nearby. One of its tinted windows lowered, but Bee couldn't see who was inside.

'...And of course Gus will live on in the memory of those who loved him.'

Bee wanted to cry, but she'd already sweated out all her available liquid. Who *had* loved Gus? Gus wasn't even a real person. Had anyone ever loved Gregory Uriel Swindon? Bee glanced towards the black car.

'Would anybody like to say a few words about Gus?'

There was an uncomfortable pause. Then Akiko Kobayashi took an uncertain step forward, her heels sinking into the grass.

'Good morning,' she said. 'Gus was...a valued employee. His contribution to the museum is much appreciated.'

Bee glanced over at Toby to find him watching her. She smiled tentatively and he looked away. She had a sudden vivid flashback to the Red Rotunda, her lips pressed against Toby's, the cold glass of the case underneath her. The case containing the horseshoe crab and...

'The deathstalker scorpion,' she murmured, as every single puzzle piece fell into place.

It was the perfect solution. But could it be possible?

Kobayashi stopped talking and turned to look at her.

'Did you want to say something, Beatrice?'

Bee felt her face go even redder. 'Um, I just wanted to say how much I enjoyed working with Gus. He was a great teacher. I learned a lot from him about animals and preparation and museums and...' A lump lodged itself in her throat. 'And...he taught me a lot about myself.' She looked over at Toby. 'He was a really amazing person. I was very lucky to know him, even if it was only for a short time. I wish I'd...appreciated him more, when he was around. I'm really going to miss him.'

She fell silent, and the celebrant nodded briskly and thanked everyone for coming. The funeral was being paid for by the museum, so there was no reception or morning tea afterwards. Kobayashi and the two preparators wandered off. Bee took a deep breath and went over to Toby.

'Hey,' she said.

'Hey.'

'Look, I'm sorry,' said Bee. 'I got caught up in detective mode. All the novels go on and on about remaining objective...but I'm not so sure that's a good idea. Anyway, I'm really, really sorry. And I know you probably hate me now, but I wanted to tell you that if, at any point, you changed your mind and wanted to...to roll a pebble at my feet, then I'd be totally up for it. Or I could roll you a pebble. Do the girl penguins roll pebbles?'

'No.'

'Well, maybe I'll roll something else,' said Bee. 'Like a... marble or a gobstopper or a glass eye.'

'What do you want, Bee?'

Bee couldn't read Toby's expression at all. There was no cheeky twinkle in his eye. That wasn't a good sign.

Bee swallowed. 'Two things. Firstly I want you to forgive me, and see if you think we can be friends again. Or more. Whatever you're comfortable with.'

'And secondly?'

'I need your help. I need you to go back to the museum, and get Kobayashi and Featherstone into the Red Rotunda. We need to do this right.'

Out of the corner of Bee's eye, she saw the window on the black car slide up as the car slowly pulled away. Bee was running out of time.

'Please,' she said to Toby. 'I need you.'

'Give me one reason why I should help you.'

Bee grabbed his hand and gave it a squeeze.

'Because I know who killed Gus.'

She leaned forward and kissed him quickly on the mouth, and before Toby had time to react, she sprinted away after the black car.

It wasn't going very fast, and she soon caught up with it. She rapped on the tinted window, which lowered. Bee looked at the old man inside. He seemed shrunken with age and sorrow, and his pale eyes looked lost and frightened, as though he wasn't quite sure what he was doing in the back seat of such an expensive car. He stared at her, concentration deepening the lines of his brow.

Bee said the old man's name, softly, and he started.

'Do you mind if I get in for a moment?' said Bee. 'I wanted to ask you about a break-in at your estate on the night of Thursday the thirteenth. Then I'd really appreciate it if you'd accompany me back to the museum so we can get this all sorted out.'

22

THE DOOR TO THE RED Rotunda was closed. Bee took a deep breath and opened it, hoping against hope that Toby had done what she'd asked.

He had. Featherstone was sitting on one of the red leather chairs in the centre of the room looking ostentatiously bored, and Kobayashi was sitting next to him, tapping her foot.

And Toby was there, standing over by the deathstalker scorpion. Bee wanted to run over and throw her arms around him. Did this mean he'd forgiven her?

William Cranston followed her into the room, and stiffened when he saw Featherstone.

'It's okay,' Bee murmured. 'This will be the last time you'll have to see him.' She shut the door behind Cranston.

Toby glanced up as they entered, but Bee couldn't tell if he was pleased to see her.

Featherstone's bored expression vanished when he saw William Cranston. His face went completely white, and his eyes widened until he resembled some kind of frightening scruffy insect. Then the look of fear vanished, and was replaced with a carefully constructed mask of disinterest.

Kobayashi examined her nails. Nobody said anything.

Bee showed William Cranston to one of the red leather chairs. He didn't say anything, or look at anyone, or betray any emotion at all. He just sat and stared at his hands, neatly folded in his lap. Bee nodded at Toby, who also took a seat.

'Right,' she said, suddenly feeling a bit stupid. 'Well, thank you all for coming.'

Was she really going to stand in front of these people and deliver a Sherlock Holmes–style explanatory speech, detailing her investigation and withholding the vital clue until the very last minute? Hadn't she learned that despite murder and betrayal and intrigue, the world *wasn't* like a detective story, and it was dangerous to treat it as one?

But here everyone was. Perhaps she should just tell them everything at once, and if they wanted more detail she could provide it. There was no point staging a whole theatrical routine around it for the sake of drama.

'This Nancy Drew crap is ridiculous,' said Kobayashi. 'I'm leaving.' She stood up.

'No,' said Bee sharply. She glared at Kobayashi. Nancy may have had annoyingly perfect hair and implausibly convenient good fortune, but *nobody* dissed her in front of Bee.

Kobayashi bristled.

'I have something to say, and you're going to listen. So sit.'

Kobayashi sat.

'Now,' said Bee. 'I'm going to start at the beginning, because that's how it's done.'

Toby gave her a look that Bee thought *might* contain the teensiest hint of a twinkle, and she felt a surge of excitement. There was something to be said for a little drama after all.

'Firstly,' said Bee. 'Firstly I have to explain about Adrian Featherstone.' She glanced at Kobayashi. 'Although I'm sure none of what I'm about to say will come as a huge surprise to anyone here.'

She told them about Featherstone's work at BioFresh, and how he had stolen research findings from Cranston. Featherstone's lip curled as Bee explained how Cranston had destroyed Featherstone's career.

'So he was left with nothing,' she said. 'Except for millions of dollars of ill-gotten gain, which dwindled away within a few years.'

Featherstone sneered, but didn't deny anything. William Cranston still didn't look up from his folded hands.

'So once all the money had been frittered away,' said Bee, 'Featherstone needed to get his hands on more. He couldn't go back to working in the sciences because Dr Cranston had muddied his name to every laboratory in the world. So he hatched a plan for revenge. He would get close to Cranston again, in whatever way he could, he would find out whatever Cranston was working on, and he would steal it and sell it. The plan had worked so well last time – how could it possibly go wrong?'

Bee looked at Featherstone, but he just raised his eyebrows at her in a patronising sort of way.

'He told me it was ironic that he got a job here, but it was actually carefully calculated. Museum sciences aren't like other sciences; they're part of a completely different sector. So nobody here would know who he was. And with this museum having close ties to Doctor Cranston, it was a perfect base of operations. And so he waited for his opportunity to arrive. Which it did – in the shape of Gus.'

Bee started to pace up and down the Red Rotunda, her hands behind her back. Despite the seriousness of the situation, she was genuinely enjoying herself.

'Although Featherstone had never met Cranston or Gus, he'd seen a picture during his dogged research of Cranston. A picture of William Cranston and his faithful assistant and friend, Gregory Uriel Swindon. And as soon as he saw Gus in the museum's taxidermy lab, he realised that Gus was, in fact, Gregory. Gus almost certainly recognised Featherstone instantly.'

Toby looked confused. 'What I don't understand is why Gus came to work at the museum in the first place. Was it just to keep tabs on Featherstone?'

'I'll get to that soon,' said Bee, flashing him a quick smile. 'So,' she continued, 'Gus was keeping an eye on Featherstone, making sure that all access to Cranston was blocked off, and ready to pounce if Featherstone tried anything dodgy. It gave Featherstone the perfect motive for murder. With Gus out of the way, the path to Cranston was clear. Let's add to this the fact that Featherstone was close to finding out what Cranston had been working on. But he also knew he was running out of time, as Cranston appeared to be nearing the end of his project.'

Kobayashi shook her head in shocked disbelief.

'Featherstone was seen in the Red Rotunda a few days before Gus died. He was agitated, like he was looking for something. Gus was found with an empty vial of mercuric chloride in his hand – a vial taken from a display case in the museum. The only person we know who had access to that case was Featherstone. Gus was also found wearing Featherstone's hoodie – with a pocketful of the old glass eyes that Featherstone had been replacing.'

'*You*,' said Kobayashi, staring at Featherstone with a look of total horror on her face. 'You promised me you didn't do it. I *helped* you…'

Adrian Featherstone opened his mouth to protest his innocence, but Bee got there first.

'No,' she said. 'It wasn't Featherstone.'

The Head Conservator looked somewhat taken aback, as if he'd been expecting Bee to accuse him.

'Of course,' Bee continued, 'Featherstone isn't really *innocent* either. He *was* trying to steal Cranston's research again, and he was planning to use Gus to get to Cranston. But you know that already.'

Kobayashi looked uncomfortable.

'But he's no murderer,' said Bee. 'He's got a pretty watertight alibi, really, although understandably not one he was willing to broadcast. Did anyone else see that news report about an attempted break-in in Healesville on the same night that Gus died? The property was Cranston's, and the would-be thief was Featherstone.'

Adrian Featherstone opened his mouth to protest.

'The street directory on your desk,' said Bee. 'Page 449. And now I've confirmed that Cranston's private security staff found a man fitting your description trying to break into Cranston's laboratory. You were apprehended but managed to get away at around 1:30 AM, just before the police arrived. There's no way you could have killed Gus.'

Cranston's head nodded slightly to confirm this, but with an air of regret, as if he wished it *had* been Featherstone.

'Of course,' said Toby to Featherstone with a somewhat malicious little grin. 'Even if you had been successful in breaking into Cranston's lab, it would've been too late.'

Featherstone's head snapped around and he stared at Toby.

'Didn't you hear?' said Toby, his grin widening. 'Cranston submitted his research a few days ago. It's really taking the scientific community by storm.'

Adrian Featherstone was as white as chalk. His face looked as though it was going to crumble into powder. 'He...published?'

'Yep. Guess you'll have to find someone else to steal ideas from,' said Toby. 'Or perhaps you should just bite the bullet and rob a bank. Or take up puppy-kicking as a hobby. To satisfy all your nasty urges.'

Featherstone seemed completely lost for words. He opened his mouth and shut it again, then made a face like he was about to be sick.

'So,' said Bee. 'As clearly demonstrated, Adrian Featherstone is a bad man. But he isn't a murderer.'

Kobayashi had a peculiar expression on her face, as it became obvious that her chances of getting a cut of Featherstone's dirty money had vanished. Disappointment flashed over her features, but was replaced with a kind of resigned relief. Kobayashi had clearly been uncomfortable with swindling the museum's great benefactor.

'Well, then,' she said, clearing her throat and trying to be businesslike. 'Can you please hurry this up? I've got an appointment at three-thirty.'

Bee turned to her and smiled. 'I'd better talk about you, then, Akiko. You, the ruthless businesswoman who would do anything to keep the museum above water. The museum would stand to benefit significantly from Cranston's death. When you heard about Cranston's illness, you started to think, *what if he died*? A great tragedy for science, certainly, but not for the museum. Then an old man called Gus turns up, with a sketchy CV and no previous employment experience to speak of, and you make him Head Taxidermist. You knew who he really was, of course. You'd seen that newspaper article too; it's how you knew Cranston was ill. You didn't let on that you knew his real name and identity, but you also knew that he was getting first dibs on Cranston's estate when Cranston died. What would happen if Gus were to unfortunately expire before Cranston?'

'Come *on*,' said Kobayashi. 'We both know I didn't do it, so let's move on.'

'Didn't you?' said Bee. 'You're pretty cunning, Akiko. You discovered what Featherstone was up to. But instead of firing him or turning him over to the cops, you made him a deal. You'd keep his secret too, but only in exchange for a cut of the profits. Cranston had been working on something pretty big – Featherstone stood to make several hundred million dollars from it. Easily enough to clear the museum of its debt.'

'Fine,' snapped Kobayashi. 'So I turned a blind eye to Featherstone. And I *may* have supplied him with some information to help him find Cranston. But I'm not a murderer, and frankly I'm sick of this.' She stood up again.

Bee grinned. She'd been waiting her whole life for this moment. 'Akiko Kobayashi,' she said, 'where were you on the night of January the thirteenth?'

'We've already had this conversation,' said Kobayashi. 'I was at home. In bed. Asleep.'

'No, you weren't,' Toby put in. 'You were at the museum. I saw you, coming out of Featherstone's office.'

Featherstone glared at Kobayashi.

'What?' she said to him with an almost hysterical laugh. 'Do you seriously think I trusted you? I knew you'd try to run off with all the money if you had a chance. I was just gathering a little...insurance to make sure you'd keep your word.'

'So, Akiko,' said Bee. 'You had a motive. You have no alibi. You were seen near the scene of the crime.'

Akiko Kobayashi was white. 'But...' she said, her voice high and panicked. 'But I didn't do it. I didn't!'

Bee paused, letting her stew for as long as possible. Then she shook her head. 'No,' she said. 'You didn't. But I think you should be a bit more careful who you associate with in the future. You're making some pretty crappy life decisions.'

Kobayashi swallowed. 'Then who killed Gus?' She turned to Cranston. 'Was it you?'

William Cranston didn't look up from his folded hands.

'Who?' asked Kobayashi. 'Who did it?'

'No one.' Bee took a deep breath. 'Gus isn't dead.'

There was a long silence in the room. Everyone stared at Bee. Toby had a strange expression on his face that was half admiration, half this-girl-is-crazy fear.

'But Bee,' he said. It was the first time he'd said her name since the cemetery. 'We *saw* him. We saw his body. It was definitely Gus.'

Bee smiled at him and dismissed the dizzy, fuzzy feeling she got when he smiled back. She had to concentrate.

'Remember the story about the boy in the car accident?' she said. 'And how the doctor was really his mother?'

Toby nodded.

'It's like that,' said Bee. 'This whole time we've been making one huge mistake. It's totally skewed our perception of what happened that night. And it's all based around one assumption. It was a totally logical assumption to make, but you should never assume anything. It's like when Sherlock Holmes said that circumstantial evidence can be misleading. Sometimes it seems like it can only mean one thing, but if you look at it another way, all the evidence suddenly points to something totally different.'

'So what's it pointing to now?'

'We all assumed that the man found dead in the Red Rotunda was Gregory Uriel Swindon, or Gus. Except it wasn't. Gregory Swindon isn't dead at all. He's right here in this room.'

Bee looked at William Cranston, who finally looked up from his folded hands, closed his eyes and nodded.

'CRANSTON WAS SICK,' SAID BEE, looking at the old man.

He nodded. 'He was dying,' he said, his voice quiet and a little shaky. 'He'd had a few cancer scares before, but last year there'd been a big one. The doctors told him he had six months to live, at the very most. That's when he came up with the whole plan.'

'Cranston never had a family,' said Bee. 'No one to carry on his name. His research was always the most important thing to him.'

'It was William's life,' said the old man. 'Losing that Nobel Prize in 1986 was like losing a child to him. It meant he'd lost his legacy. His name could never be carried on by children, so he wanted it to at least live on in scientific history. That's why he donated all this.' He looked around the Red Rotunda. 'So at least he'd be remembered in here.'

'So he kept trying for another Nobel,' said Bee. 'He kept researching, and then he found it. The deathstalker scorpion.'

Toby shook his head in amazement. 'Chlorotoxins,' he said. 'All of that time we spent in there looking at dogs' eyes and horseshoe crabs, the answer was there all along – just in a different part of the case.'

'Cranston discovered that its venom contains a neurotoxin that might be a cure for cancer,' explained Bee.

Kobayashi snapped to attention. 'What?' she said. 'Cranston had a cure for cancer?'

Toby shrugged. 'He certainly had the first steps,' he said. 'He'd done all the groundwork. There's a long way to go, but the major breakthrough has been made.'

Kobayashi glanced at Featherstone, who was staring stubbornly at the floor.

'Didn't he mention that, Akiko?' asked Bee. 'He didn't tell you the thing you were stealing from Cranston was a cure for cancer? Do you see what I was saying before about life choices?'

Kobayashi swallowed and didn't respond.

'So Cranston had found it,' Bee continued. 'He'd made the breakthrough that was going to cement his legacy. He was just a hair's-breadth away from finally getting his Nobel Prize. There were just two things in his way.'

Adrian Featherstone shifted his weight uncomfortably.

Bee smiled at him. 'That's right,' she said. 'You were the first thing. But Cranston didn't really see you as much of a threat. He was much more careful with security, made sure that none of his staff got too close or stayed long enough to really figure out what he was doing. The only person he confided in was his closest friend and assistant, Gregory. Or Gus, as we knew him.'

'So what was the second thing in his way?' asked Kobayashi.

'Death,' said Bee. 'Cranston was dying. His doctors told him he had no more than six months to live. The Nobel Prize nominations aren't until September.'

'And?'

'And you can't win a Nobel Prize if you're dead.'

'That's right,' Toby confirmed. 'You can win it if you're still alive when nominated, but there are no posthumous nominations.' He turned to the old man in the red leather chair. 'Oh,' he said, realisation creeping across his face.

'William hung on for as long as he could,' said the old man. 'He was very sick, but he still came to work every day and pretended everything was all right. He was in a lot of pain by the end. But he had to make sure everything was ready. He wanted to make sure everything was in place, before he . . .' The old man turned his head away.

Bee smiled sadly. 'And that's why he ate so much junk food the day he died,' she said. 'Because it was all ready.'

The old man laughed bitterly. 'He'd been stuck on a macrobiotic diet of brown rice and seaweed for six months in the hope that it might give him more time. I used to find him staring at recipe books, at pictures of cakes and roast beef and fried chicken.'

Toby was shaking his head. 'So he *did* kill himself,' he said. 'After all that, it *was* a suicide.'

Bee nodded. 'Occam's razor,' she said. 'I told you so. The simplest explanation is always the most likely.'

'Except this is hardly simple.'

'Nothing ever is.'

Toby held Bee's gaze for a long moment, and Bee's insides squirmed happily.

Kobayashi was staring at the old man. 'You're not William Cranston,' she said, slowly.

'Well done,' snapped Featherstone. 'Only took you ten minutes longer than everyone else in the room.'

'Shut up,' she said. 'You used to *work* for him, and you didn't figure it out.'

Featherstone shut his mouth and resumed his sulky floor-staring.

Bee pulled the newspaper article out of her pocket. 'I should have realised,' she said. 'William Cranston was known for being a recluse. Yet here I was thinking it was *him* who was grinning at the camera, and Gus – Gregory – who was looking shyly down at the ground.' She pointed at the caption on the photo. 'And it says "Scientist and Museum Benefactor William Cranston with his assistant, Gregory Uriel Swindon". Not the other way around. It's *Cranston* standing on the left, not Gus. *Cranston* is the one with the dark eyes. Those pale blue eyes belong to Gregory.'

She looked into the old man's eyes. Not smiling and sparkling like they had been in the photo, but sad and bloodshot. But they were as startlingly pale as ever.

'I kept looking for clues relating to reptile eyes,' said Bee. 'But it was human eyes I should have been paying attention to.'

'We swapped,' said the old man. 'It was William's idea, of course. I didn't want to do it. I didn't want him to die. I didn't want to be responsible for his death, or for seeing out his legacy. I didn't want to give up who I was, even though I was no one special. But he wore me down, and in the end I couldn't refuse a dying man's last request. Especially not his. Nobody had seen him for thirty years, and one old man looks much like another. It was easier than we thought. He became Gus, and came here to work at the museum that he loved so much. Taxidermy

293

had always been a hobby of his, it just made sense. We thought six months would be long enough to establish his identity. Then it was time.'

'But why the mercuric chloride?' asked Kobayashi.

'It wasn't mercuric chloride,' said Bee. 'That vial was full of water. It was a backup plan, in case anyone doubted that Gus had committed suicide. The only other person who could have got hold of that vial was Featherstone, and if he was implicated in Gus's death...' She shrugged.

'He'd deserve it,' growled Gregory Uriel Swindon, with a black look at Featherstone.

'So how *did* he do it?' asked Kobayashi. 'If it wasn't the mercuric chloride, how *did* Gus... Cranston kill himself?'

'It was the venom of the deathstalker scorpion,' said Toby. 'Wasn't it?' He looked at the old man.

'William was always the researcher,' said Gregory Swindon. 'He wanted to record the effects of the venom on a human – a sick human. He wanted to see how long death would take after administering the venom – how long you could safely wait before administering antivenom, and whether that would be enough time for the chlorotoxins to destroy cancerous cells.'

Toby looked interested. 'And was it?'

'I don't know,' admitted Swindon. 'I'm no scientist. I just recorded the findings and will forward them to the relevant people.'

'You'd been planning it for a while, hadn't you?' said Bee. 'Gus – William Cranston – swiped the mercuric chloride bottle months ago, and then two weeks ago he borrowed the key to the Red Rotunda and had a copy made. You made sure people saw you in the Red Rotunda, and associated your face with the name of William Cranston. On the night itself, Cranston stayed in the office until 8:37 and then hid somewhere, I assume with you.' She looked at Swindon, who nodded.

'I was waiting by the staff entry just before closing,' he said. 'William let me in and I waited in one of the store-rooms. He joined me later on, and we waited until after midnight, so we could be sure everyone had gone home.'

'Except we hadn't,' said Bee.

'We actually didn't know that,' said Gregory Swindon. 'William had left his smartcard in the taxidermy lab. When he popped back in to get it, he saw the door to the Catacombs open and the light on. He never imagined there was someone in there, but being the meticulous man he was, he had to turn off the light and close the door. Then he picked up your watch.' He nodded at Bee. 'We borrowed your watch. Sorry. In all our months of planning, neither of us remembered to bring a watch. Then we went upstairs.'

Bee blinked. They had taken her watch? She hadn't even noticed it was missing. She'd been so busy trying to remember if Gus's smartcard had been on his desk when she and Toby had come out of the Catacombs she hadn't thought about what *else* might be missing.

'You went to the Red Rotunda,' Toby was saying.

'William wanted to die among his past, his research. It was the closest he could get to dying surrounded by family.'

'And you,' said Bee. 'He wanted his best friend there to help him record the data. Researching until the end.'

'Yes.' Gregory Swindon's face crumpled. 'He had the deathstalker venom ready in a syringe. He got me to set the watch at midnight exactly, and then injected himself. It didn't take long for him to die.' He sighed. 'Eleven minutes and twenty-four seconds, to be precise. When he was gone, I slipped the mercuric chloride into his hand, took his smartcard and the syringe, and went back to the lab. I reset your watch according to the clock on the wall and replaced it.'

Bee let a bubble of surprised laughter escape. 'I kept wondering why the clock on the wall was suddenly correct.

But it was actually my watch that was now three minutes slow as well.'

'How did you get out of the building?' asked Toby, looking at Swindon.

'First I went back to the storeroom. I waited until the next morning, when more people would be moving around the museum and my departure wouldn't attract the attention of Security. Then I slipped out, threw away the smartcard and the syringe, and sat down on a bench in the sunshine, trying to comprehend what I'd just done.'

Bee remembered seeing him as Toby was dragging her off to the café across the road.

'And that's really all,' said Gregory Swindon. 'Nothing that complicated. Just an old man who wanted to die, but not be forgotten.'

He looked back down at his hands and closed his eyes. Bee saw his shoulders tremble.

'Well,' said Adrian Featherstone, standing up. 'That was all very enlightening. Now if you'll excuse me...'

'Not so fast,' said Toby. 'I'm not sure we've quite dealt with the issue of you and what a terribly bad man you are.'

Featherstone smirked. 'It doesn't matter anyway. William Cranston is dead. It's not as though I can steal his work now.'

'And yet I don't really feel like justice has been served.' Toby shook his head.

'So what?' snarled Featherstone. 'It's not like you can touch me. If you expose me to the authorities, I'll just tell them the truth about William Cranston, and then there'll be no Nobel Prize. No legacy. No history books. And you've all got too much to hide. *You* can't risk your secret coming out,' he said, nodding at Gregory Swindon. 'And *you* were working with me,' he sneered at Kobayashi. 'You're just as guilty as I am.'

'What about us?' asked Toby, going over and standing next to Bee. '*We* have nothing to lose.'

'You?' Featherstone barked out a short laugh. 'You're just a couple of kids. As if anyone's going to believe your crazy harebrained story over the sensible, pragmatic word of a respected conservator.'

'Hmm,' said Toby. 'I'm afraid I might have some bad news for you.'

'What?' said Featherstone with mock terror. 'Are you going to dob me in to your mummy? You can't go to the police. There's no evidence against me that would stand up in a court of law.'

'I have no intention of turning you over to the police,' said Toby. 'The people I'm working for have much more… scientific methods of exacting justice.'

'The *people you work for*?' said Featherstone, laughing shrilly. 'What are you, a superhero?'

'Hardly,' said Toby. 'But does the name Patrick Meagher mean anything to you?'

Adrian Featherstone stopped laughing.

'He's my dean at uni,' Toby explained. 'We're pretty good mates, actually. It was Patrick who suggested I come here to get some work experience. And he had a couple of little jobs for me while I was here, some stuff for this club he belongs to. It's called the Royal Society and from what I hear it's pretty awesome.'

Adrian Featherstone looked nervously towards the door.

'You can run, Featherstone,' said Toby with a grin. 'Feel free to leave any time you like. But they'll find you. Your confession to me just now is more than enough for them. They will find you, and I have no idea what they'll do to you, but I know they're a pretty creative, intelligent bunch of people. Always inventing new ways to do things.'

Featherstone fled the room, skidding on the parquetry floor as he left.

'Have a lovely day,' called Toby, as the door banged shut.

Kobayashi had risen rather nervously to her feet. 'So what happens now?'

'Well,' said Bee, cocking her head to one side. 'I'm

pretty sure that Featherstone won't be coming back, so you'll have to find a new Head Conservator.'

Kobayashi gulped. 'So you're not going to...'

'Dob you in?' asked Bee. 'No. Not as long as you don't mention any of this to anyone.' She looked at Gregory Swindon. 'William Cranston deserves his Nobel Prize, don't you think?'

Kobayashi nodded. 'I won't say anything.'

'Thank you,' said the old man. 'And as I'm now in control of William's finances, I shall make sure the museum will overcome its financial difficulties.'

Toby raised his eyebrows. 'Are you sure she deserves that?'

'William loved this museum,' said Gregory Swindon. 'I'd hate to see it replaced by another ice-skating rink or shopping complex.'

Kobayashi whispered a hoarse 'thank you', and then quietly left the room. Bee turned to Swindon, who stood up slowly.

'Thanks for coming,' she said. 'I think Cranston's research will be safe from Featherstone now.'

'Thank you,' said Swindon. 'William always liked you. He told me all about you.'

'Really?'

Swindon nodded. 'He said you were the perfect assistant, and that your back-and-forth stitch was the best he'd ever seen.'

Bee felt a lump in her throat. Gregory Swindon shook her hand, and Toby's.

'Good luck,' said Bee. 'With the Nobel Prize and everything.'

Swindon inclined his head, and then shuffled from the room.

Bee gave Toby a hesitant smile. He didn't smile back. Maybe he hadn't forgiven her after all. Bee wondered if she should grovel.

'Um,' she said.

Toby scratched his nose. 'Look,' he said. 'Before you start whatever speech you've got planned, I think you should let me make something clear.'

That didn't sound good. Grovelling was definitely now an option. 'But I need to apolog—'

'No,' he said. He grabbed her shoulders and held her in place. 'You're going to *listen*.'

'But—'

Toby had no hands free to put over Bee's mouth, so he leaned in and kissed her. The kiss was warm and soft, but firm. It was a kiss that said *shut up*, and Bee shut up. For quite some time.

When they finally broke apart, Toby nodded briskly. 'Any comments? Questions?'

Bee found she couldn't quite manage speaking. Her knees felt rather trembly, and she was glad Toby was still holding her by the shoulders.

'You're very clever, do you know that?' Toby smiled at Bee, and to her utter joy she saw that the twinkle was back in full force.

'Yes,' said Bee. 'Yes, I do. But I couldn't have done it without you, Watson.'

Toby grinned and kissed the top of her head. 'Come on,' he said. 'Let's go and tell Faro Costa that we banished the shadows.'

24

THE TAXIDERMY LAB SEEMED SOMEHOW smaller. Bee gathered the few things that she'd left at her desk, and tidied away the tools and scraps of cottonwool and wire. The completed animals had been carefully wrapped and boxed and were ready to be taken to the exhibition space, where the curators would pose them in glass cases and write carefully worded cards with the animals' Latin names and some information about habitats and diets. Bee thought about all that those animals had witnessed over the last two weeks, and wondered what the cards would say if she were in charge of writing them.

'Well,' said Toby, when every last pair of tweezers had been put away.

Bee reached up to the third shelf from the right and four shelves down, and screwed a lid onto the jar marked EYES, REPTILE, S–M.

'Well,' she replied.

Toby's mouth curled in a crooked smile. 'Is hanging out with you always this intense?'

Bee laughed. 'I hope not,' she said. 'At least, not with the death and danger and intrigue. Not all the time, anyway.'

'But there'll still be a *bit* of intensity, right?'

Bee leaned in and kissed him. It was supposed to be a soft and gentle kiss, but it very quickly got out of hand. Bee felt Toby's shirt under her hands, and under that, the warmth of his chest and the fast thumping of his heart. She felt his mouth smile, and she pulled away.

'Intensity,' said Toby, breathing heavily. 'Check.'

① ① ①

Bee arrived home later – quite a bit later – to find Angela and Neal sitting at the dining-room table playing Settlers of Catan. Angela stood up when Bee entered the room.

'Are you okay?' said Angela, coming over and giving Bee a hug. 'You left so suddenly this morning and you haven't been answering your phone all day.'

'I'm fine,' said Bee. 'Actually, I'm good.'

Angela squeezed her. 'I'm sorry if I haven't been around much to talk to.'

'It's fine, really.'

'What's been going on? Why were you so upset this morning?'

Bee considered telling her mother the whole story, but the thought exhausted her. She'd already been through it once that day. She'd tell Angela some other time.

'You know,' said Bee. 'The funeral. Everything. But everything's fine now.'

'Promise?'

'Promise.'

Angela gave Bee one last hug and kissed her cheek, before sitting back down at the table. The Celestial Badger looked up at Bee and smiled.

'Oh,' said Bee, smiling back at him. 'And I wanted to say thanks, Neal. For your advice last night. You were right. I did just need a good night's rest.'

The Celestial Badger's smile broke into a grin, and Bee thought that maybe he wasn't *so* awkward-looking after all. 'You're welcome,' he said.

'Do you have any plans for tonight?' Angela asked Bee. 'We were going to order takeaway and watch DVDs.'

Bee grinned. 'That sounds like the best night ever.'

Angela looked pleased. 'Do you have any pizza preferences?' she asked, standing up to get the menu. 'You should pick, as it's your last night of freedom.'

'Nope,' said Bee. 'You choose. I have to do a couple of things first, then I'll be ready for whatever your DVD collection wants to throw at me.'

On top of Bee's wardrobe there was a large cardboard box. She stood on a chair and dragged the box down. It was heavy, and covered with dust. Bee sneezed. Then she sat down on her bed and summed up.

1. Toby liked her. *Liked* liked her.
2. She liked him back.
3. A lot.
4. More than she'd ever liked Fletch.
5. It was possible that Toby wanted to be her boyfriend.
6. This was a nice thought.
7. If Bee had a boyfriend, she didn't have to feel hurt about Fletch dumping her.
8. And people wouldn't feel sorry for her. Especially if her new boyfriend was a hot genius PhD student.
9. If she wasn't angry or sad about Fletch, then she didn't mind if he had a new girlfriend.
10. Like Maddy.
11. She missed Maddy.
12. And technically Bee had cheated on Fletch as well. Sort of.

13. So technically *he* hadn't dumped *her*. They'd just *broken up*.

14. Which meant Maddy hadn't stolen her boyfriend.

15. Which meant she didn't have to be mad at Maddy.

Bee looked at the phone lying on her desk. Had the Celestial Badger been right? Could it really just be a case of getting over it and calling Maddy? Could everything just go back to normal? Friendship was supposed to be such a complicated thing; surely it couldn't be that simple.

She wondered what William of Ockham would have advised her to do. Would he have said the same thing as the Celestial Badger?

Bee thought about Toby, and that funny half-smiling look he got just before he kissed her. Something happy and fizzy bubbled up inside her, and she wanted to *tell* someone.

She wanted to tell Maddy.

Bee picked up her phone and scrolled down her contacts list.

Maddy answered, sounding surprised. 'Bee?'

'Hey.'

'Hey yourself!' Maddy sounded pleased and nervous. 'How are you?'

'I'm good,' said Bee, and was surprised to find out it was true. 'Really good, actually.'

'I'm glad.' Maddy paused. 'Did you get my email?'

'Yep,' said Bee. 'Thanks. For explaining everything.'

'Oh! That's okay, you're welcome. Um. I'm sorry. Again.'

'Forget it,' said Bee. 'It really isn't important.' This, also, seemed to be true. 'So. Are you ready for school tomorrow?'

Maddy groaned. 'Yes,' she said. 'No. I don't know. I kind of want school to just get it over with, you know? Like ripping off a bandaid. Everyone's been going on and on at me all summer about what a *big deal* Year Twelve is. I just want the suspense to be over.'

'I know,' said Bee, who felt she had had quite enough suspense for one year, and it wasn't even February yet.

There was another somewhat awkward pause.

'How was your summer?' asked Maddy at last.

Bee grinned and propped her feet up on the dusty cardboard box. 'You wouldn't believe me if I told you,' she said.

William of Ockham had sort of been onto something, Bee concluded half an hour later. The simplest answer was often the right one. But simple wasn't the same thing as boring. Simple could still take your breath away. Some of the most beautiful things in the world were beautiful *because* of their simplicity. Simple things were deceptive and amazing because behind them were millions of layers of meaning and complexity, all hidden beneath the facade of simplicity.

They were the best kinds of mysteries, after all. The ones where you were completely stumped by the whole thing, along with Sherlock and Nancy and Trixie and Hercule. Until the end where everything fell into place and you couldn't believe you'd been so blind, that you hadn't seen how *simple* it all really was.

Bee remembered her eleventh birthday. It had been the first year she hadn't received a card from her father. When she was really little, he'd sent gifts, which had dwindled to cards. Then, nothing. That was when reality had sunk in. Bee had boxed up all her childish mystery novels, marched down to the library and borrowed as much adult crime as her library card would permit. She stopped making up outlandish stories about how Mr Lee was really a millionaire posing as a poor, cardigan-wearing maths teacher because his cruel ex-wife was trying to have him murdered so she could steal his fortune. She had crawled into bed after eating too much cake with her mum and Maddy, and curled up into a ball of misery. No birthday card. No mystery. Nothing. Bee had cracked the spine on a PD James novel and concluded that this must be what being a grown-up meant, and that she would just have to suck it up and deal with it.

So she did.

Until now.

Bee grabbed a pair of scissors and cut through the brown packing tape of the cardboard box. She sneezed again as she lifted the flaps open, and felt a thrill of nostalgia and recognition. It was like discovering old friends who had never really gone away.

She pulled out *The Murder of Roger Ackroyd* with its dreadful illustration of Hercule Poirot on the cover. Next came a red hardcover edition of *The Hound of the Baskervilles*. Bee flipped to the end and saw the purple stains on the paper, where she'd become so excited she'd knocked over her glass of grape juice. The copy of Agatha Christie's *Sleeping Murder* had lost its cover long ago and the pages were held together with crumbling sticky tape. Nancy Drew emerged from the box in two copies of *The Whispering Statue*, both the 1937 version and the revised 1970s version with its completely different plot. Bee paused over *Trixie Belden and the Mystery of the Headless Horseman*, remembering how thrilled she'd been when, in an almost postmodern twist, a quote from Sherlock Holmes had provided Trixie with the solution to the puzzle of the fruit trees.

Finally, at the bottom of the box, Bee found her detective kit, complete with notebook, rubber gloves, magnifying glass and lipstick. She flicked through the notebook, laughing at her outlandish feats of imagination and clumsy handwriting.

'Bee?' Angela called from the kitchen. 'The pizza's here. We're going to watch that episode of *Doctor Who* where Agatha Christie goes missing and there's a giant wasp.'

Bee grinned. 'Coming.'

The rubber gloves were starting to crumble, the thin latex unable to stand the test of time. Bee dropped them into the bin, then slid the notebook, magnifying glass and lipstick into her handbag.

Just because the world was simple, it didn't mean there wasn't any room for the occasional mystery.

Acknowledgements

First and foremost I must thank the people at Allen & Unwin – in particular Jodie Webster and Hilary Reynolds – for being so utterly delightful to work with, and for making such wonderful books with my name on the front.

Of course the whole book would be a confusing jumble of contradictions if it weren't for the storylining genius of Sarah Dollard, who is the best critic and friend a girl could wish for. As always, Justine Larbalestier also provided generous, useful and invaluable feedback.

Thanks also to Colleen Boyle for giving me a behind-the-scenes tour of the Melbourne Museum and telling me lots of disgusting stories; to Liz Hills and Chris Miles for help with D&D stuff, my dad for telling me about the snails in Patricia Highsmith's bosom, and Jess West for letting me borrow her Celestial Badger.

Mary Roach's stomach-turningly-wonderful *Stiff* taught me a lot of creepy things about death and decay that made their way into this story – it's a highly recommended read.

And, finally, to my oldest friend, Anna Grace Hopkins – thanks for sticking around.

About the author

LILI WILKINSON WAS BORN IN Melbourne, Australia, in the front room where her parents still live. She was first published when she was twelve, in *Voiceworks* magazine. After studying Creative Arts at Melbourne University, Lili worked on insideadog.com.au, the Inky Awards and the Inkys Creative Reading Prize at the Centre for Youth Literature, State Library of Victoria. She now spends most of her time reading and writing books for teenagers. She's won awards for the writing part, but not the reading, unless you count the stopwatch she won once in the MS Readathon.

Lili's other books include:
Pink
Angel Fish
The (Not Quite) Perfect Boyfriend
Scatterheart
Joan of Arc